'*Into The Dark Forest* is packed full of the best
kind of magic – I want to be a Wildsmith!'
DAISY MAY JOHNSON

'Liz has crafted a stunningly rich world and
characters – brimming with magic and wonder,
yet wonderfully warm and familiar. The lush
illustrations feel reminiscent of the beautiful
animations of Studio Ghibli.'
GABRIELLE KENT

'Sneak inside the wonderful world of the Wildsmith,
and take a peek at the secrets and magic, that lay
hidden, deep within an enchanted fairytale forest.
This is a fantastic first chapter book which will delight
young fans of magic, animals, and adventure.'
HARRY HEAPE

HAVE YOU EVER WONDERED HOW BOOKS ARE MADE?

UCLAN PUBLISHING is an award-winning independent publisher, specialising in Children's and Young Adult books. Based at The University of Central Lancashire, this Preston-based publisher teaches MA Publishing students how to become industry professionals using the content and resources from its business; students are included at every stage of the publishing process and credited for the work that they contribute.

The business doesn't just help publishing students though. UCLan Publishing has supported the employability and real-life work skills for the University's Illustration, Acting, Translation, Animation, Photography, Film & TV students and many more. This is the beauty of books and stories; they fuel many other creative industries! The MA Publishing

WILDSMITH

INTO THE DARK FOREST

Praise for *Wildsmith: Into the Dark Forest*

'A lush, rich, page-turning adventure from
one of the most versatile writers we have.
There's no genre Liz can't write in.'
PHIL EARLE

'*Wildsmith* has everything I want in a story –
magic, mystery and dragons! Liz is the mistress
of dragons and in this thrilling adventure she has
cast her story-telling spell with utter charm and
skill. Children are in for such a treat! Thank
goodness there's a sequel – I want more!'
JASBINDER BILAN

'Wildsmiths, dragons, witches and the protection of
magical animals! What's not to love? An enchanting
read. Beautifully written and utterly charming.
I can't wait for the next adventure!'
ELOISE WILLIAMS

students are able to get involved from day one with the business and they acquire a behind the scenes experience of what it is like to work for a such a reputable independent.

The MA course was awarded a Times Higher Award (2018) for Innovation in the Arts and the business, UCLan Publishing was awarded Best Newcomer at the Independent Publishing Guild (2019) for the ethos of teaching publishing using a commercial publishing house. As the business continues to grow, so too does the student experience upon entering this dynamic Masters course.

www.uclanpublishing.com
www.uclanpublishing.com/courses/
uclanpublishing@uclan.ac.uk

Also available by Liz Flanagan

Eden Summer

Legends of the Sky series
Dragon Daughter
Rise of the Shadow Dragons

Wildsmith series
Wildsmith: Into the Dark Forest
Wildsmith: City of Secrets

LIZ FLANAGAN

Illustrated by Joe Todd-Stanton

WILDSMITH

INTO THE DARK FOREST

uclan publishing

Wildsmith: Into the Dark Forest is a uclanpublishing book

First published in Great Britain in 2023 by
uclanpublishing
University of Central Lancashire
Preston, PR1 2HE, UK

978-1-915235-04-6

1 3 5 7 9 10 8 6 4 2

Set in 12/19pt Kingfisher by Becky Chilcott.

A CIP catalogue record for this book is available from the British Library.

Printed and bound in Great Britain by Clays Ltd, Elcograf S.p.A.

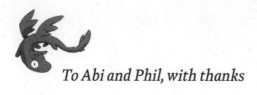 *To Abi and Phil, with thanks*

CHAPTER ONE

O N THE MORNING HER LIFE TURNED UPSIDE down, all Rowan could think about was the race against her best friend, Bella. None of the other children were as quick as them. This race would prove who knew the city's secrets best, who was fastest and most agile. They lined up just inside the city walls, both determined to win today, as they waited for the bell to chime the hour.

'Your hand isn't even touching the door!' Rowan complained. 'You know the rules, and that one was your idea.'

'It's covered in cobwebs, yuck!' Bella reached out her fingers, barely grazing the huge wooden door with its rusty iron hinges. 'I don't even know why they have a door – it's always open.'

Rowan wanted to giggle at her friend's expression, but she faced forwards, planning her route through the streets of Holderby, all the way to the lookout tower in the palace gardens. 'No cheating this time – your feet mustn't touch the ground, right?' That rule was hers – it made it more interesting.

'It wasn't the ground, it was Milo!' Bella laughed. She'd won her last race by using her brother as a way of crossing a tricky section of open street.

The bell rang out, chiming the hour.

'Go!' Rowan gasped, and they both sprang into action.

Rowan climbed up the city wall to the east, using uneven stones as handholds, then pulling herself up onto a flat roof. From there, it was easy enough to tiptoe along the row of shops and houses. She knew where she was by the smells floating up: past the bakery with its

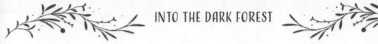

delicious steam; round the back of the forge, avoiding the iron blast of heat rising up; trying not to breathe as she passed the tannery with the stink of drying leathers. Some people waved; others ignored her; and the grumpy butcher muttered about wildcat children with nothing better to do.

She didn't look up, focusing purely on her next move. She came to the end of the street. This was the hard part: it was too far to jump across the street, but she had gambled on having help. A cart was coming along, piled with straw bales, heading for her father in the palace stables, just as she'd hoped – right on time. As it drew level, she leapt out, landed on the cart, and rolled, feeling the scratchy straw through her worn linen tunic.

'Oi, you. Cheeky! Get off my cart!' the driver yelled at her.

'Thanks!' Rowan scrambled to her feet, judging the moment perfectly, and then jumped off the other side onto a high stone wall. This was the hard part.

Her hand grabbed a stone, but it was loose. It came

right out of the wall, crashing onto her leg and smashing down onto the track below.

'Ouch!' She'd have a fine bruise on that leg tomorrow. She dangled by the other hand, feet scrabbling. She couldn't fall now!

Gritting her teeth, gripping hard till her fingers burned, Rowan pulled herself back up onto the top of the wall.

Panting, she looked around. Finally! Rowan was near her home now – the airy rooms above the stable block. She took her favourite shortcut through the palace gardens, keeping to the walls, never touching the ground. She'd even played this game with the prince himself once. He was younger and he'd fallen in the fishpond trying to catch her. She'd delivered him safely home, happy, grubby, slightly damp but quite unhurt.

Her lips curved in a smile. She was going to win today! She hoisted herself up an apple tree, darted along a high wall covered in ivy, and there was the lookout tower itself. She reached up and began to climb.

This morning the sky was blue, and the sun warmed her back as she went steadily higher.

She was almost at the top, when she heard voices and realised that the lookout tower was already occupied.

And not by Bella.

CHAPTER TWO

H-OH. ROWAN STOPPED CLIMBING, ALMOST at the top of the lookout tower. She couldn't afford to be spotted by the guards and thrown out now. She would have to wait for them to leave.

She clung on to the old stones with her hands and feet. Her arms started to ache. Her legs began to shake. *Hurry up*, she thought, as she waited.

Two grown-ups were talking, about boring things she'd heard before: some far-away war, waged by a country called Estria. She didn't know what that had

to do with them – there was no war here in Gallren.

Rowan stopped listening, watching a pigeon soar down and land in the gardens below, where there was a little dovecote. This bird had a message tied to its leg – she could see the tiny roll of paper from here.

You look tired, she thought to the pigeon. *I hope you can rest now.*

It cocked its head and looked straight at her, as if it had heard. Then Sam, the pigeon boy, ran out to take the message off and give the bird some well-deserved food and water.

'When will Kaine Stonelaw's army reach us?' a woman's voice said, in the tower above her.

'Any day now. I'm expecting a note from our border guards,' a man answered.

The first person said, 'Stonelaw thinks he can just reach out and take my country next? Not without a fight. Gallren will not give up.'

'We don't have much time,' the man said. 'Where will you go?'

'Oh, I'm not leaving!' the woman replied.

'Your Majesty, we must keep you safe.'

Your Majesty? Rowan almost fell off the tower, but she pushed her toes between the stones even harder and managed to hang on. She was eavesdropping on the queen! There were probably punishments for that.

She peered over her shoulder for Bella, so she could warn her to stay away, but there was no sign of her friend yet.

'I won't abandon my people,' the queen was saying. 'If I'm asking them to fight back and defend us, I must be here. Whatever happens.'

'At least send the prince away,' the other person suggested.

'No.' The queen sounded stubborn, her mind made up. 'What message does that send? That we are

cowards? No. We are staying right here in Holderby. I know you will keep us all safe.'

The other person sighed. 'We will do our best, Your Majesty, but war with Estria is coming.'

'And our soldiers are the finest and the bravest,' Queen Silvana said, firmly.

After a few moments, the two of them walked away, still talking, and Rowan got a clear view of the queen in her long velvet cloak, and the general, in his smart hat and uniform.

War was coming. Here? To her city? Though the sun still blazed down, Rowan suddenly felt freezing cold.

CHAPTER THREE

NSTEAD OF CLIMBING UP THE TOWER, NOW Rowan hurried back down into the gardens, ignoring the cramp in her fingers. Then she rushed to her father in the palace stables where he worked. This was her favourite place: with its warm sweet smell of horses and fresh hay. Dad said she had a gift with the horses and she'd got very good at helping him without getting underfoot.

'Dad!' She glanced over her shoulder to check the stable yard was empty. 'I was climbing, and I didn't mean to listen, but I heard the queen. What's happening?

Will there be a war? Here?' Her questions tumbled out, one after the other.

Her father was big and strong and scared of no one. She expected him to laugh and tell her it was nothing. But he didn't.

Instead, he crouched down on the cobbles, so he could look Rowan in the eye. He took her hand and said softly, 'You shouldn't have found out like that. But yes – if the rumours are true, war is coming to Gallren. It might even reach us here in Holderby.'

Just then a loud alarm bell sounded. She'd never heard this noise before. The harsh clanging rang out across the city.

'That's the sign: the fighting will reach us soon.' Her father frowned. 'Your mother and I have planned for this. The two of you must leave. Today.'

'No! I don't want to go!' Rowan threw herself at her father and hugged him tightly. She could feel his bristly beard against the top of her head. 'This is our home. I'm not leaving.' She could be brave, like the queen. 'Wait. The *two of us*? What about you?'

But her father gently unfastened her hands and held them in his huge fists. 'I don't want you to leave either.' His face was serious and sad. 'But you and your mother are going to stay with your grandpa. You will be safer there, with him.'

'What? My grandpa? What grandpa?' Rowan cried. She'd always thought she didn't have grandparents. 'Who is he? Why didn't you tell me about him before?' she asked urgently, but she could tell her father wasn't listening.

That loud clanging bell got in the way of thinking. Rowan felt as if her whole body was an alarm bell, ringing away. Her heart was galloping and her breath coming fast. Questions and worries swirled together in her mind.

'Hurry, you have to go and pack. We don't have much time.' And he stood up again. 'Here's your mother now.'

'Can't I say goodbye to Bella?' she asked. 'I was just with her. She'll wonder what happened . . .'

'No, Rowan. We are leaving right now.' One glance

LIZ FLANAGAN

at her mother's face told Rowan she had no choice. Her mother was usually cheerful and calm, in her bright clothes, with her long chestnut hair in a plait down her back. Not today. The look on her mother's face made Rowan more fearful than ever.

Rowan listened to her parents making hurried plans: which horse they'd take, and which road was the best. She felt trapped in a bad dream, but this was actually happening. Somehow she managed to do as her mother said. She stumbled back home, rolled up a bundle of clothes and packed a small bag of her most precious things: a lucky feather, a shiny pebble and her treasured book, all about animals.

They loaded up a cart and harnessed the steady chestnut carthorse called Peanut. The chestnut mare turned and whiffled comfortingly at Rowan, as if to say:

don't worry, you're safe with me. Rowan stroked Peanut's velvet nose in thanks.

And then came the worst moment: saying goodbye to Dad.

'Why can't you come too?' she said, trying not to cry.

'My job is here,' he said. 'I'll be needed more than ever.' He hugged both of them at once.

Rowan had one arm round her mother; the other round her father. This was her family. The three of them. Not some grandfather she'd never even met. She wouldn't let go of Dad, she wouldn't. Then he'd have to come with them.

But Rowan's father lifted her gently to sit on the raised seat of the cart, next to her mother. 'Be brave, my Rowan.' He gave her one last kiss on the cheek and stepped away.

As the world blurred with tears, Rowan saw her mother wipe her own eyes, sniff hard, and lift the reins.

Then they were going.

The streets were packed: the air was full of shouting and crying and farewells, as people hurried to leave before the Estrian army reached Holderby.

Rowan sat without speaking, huddled under her cloak. She still couldn't believe they were leaving it all: their friends, their home, her father.

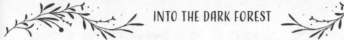 

As they passed through the city gates, she saw two guards struggling with the huge wooden doors, pushing them closed.

How could her whole life change so much in just one day?

CHAPTER FOUR

THEY ARRIVED AT GRANDPA'S HOUSE LATE at night. Rowan jerked awake, feeling stiff and cold.

Peanut shook her head, making the harness jingle. Rowan's mother jumped down, calling softly, 'Dad?'

Rowan looked around in shock. She was used to Holderby, to busy streets and houses packed tightly. There was always noise and light in the city. Here it was silent, apart from the wind stirring in the trees beyond the house. But then an owl hooted, making her jump.

Next she heard a distant rumbling noise. Could it be thunder?

Rowan looked up at the sky: it was so dark it made her eyes feel strange and empty. The only light was the moon and a sprinkling of stars. But the more she stared, the more stars she saw.

'What was that sound?' she whispered. 'It can't be thunder – there are no storm clouds, just clear sky and stars. Oh, look at the stars!'

But her mother only answered, 'We are here! This is your grandpa's house. Jump down now.' She was already striding up the stairs to the door, calling eagerly: 'Dad? Are you there?'

'Hmmph.' Rowan knew when grown-ups were avoiding her questions. She made herself a promise to find out exactly what that noise had been. She needed to explore and find out all about this new place.

As her eyes got used to the dark, Rowan could see more clearly. Grandpa's house was built between two massive tree trunks, and seemed to be growing right out of the forest. It had a steep tiled roof,

with a little window tucked in the eaves beneath the chimney.

She could hear her mother saying, 'Oh! It's so good to see you!'

Rowan breathed in, smelling woodsmoke and damp-ness and moss. And then she squeaked, as a nose nudged her hand. She looked down: seeing a huge furry head, and two bright golden eyes and pricked ears and—

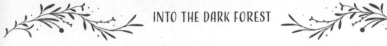
'*Wolf*!' she shrieked.

She was dazzled then, as someone lifted a lantern to her face. Too bright! She squinted up.

Rowan saw a craggy face with brown eyes twinkling down at her, under bushy white eyebrows. Beneath a thick white beard, there was a wide smile.

'Grandpa?' she managed to say, swaying with tiredness.

'Who else would it be?' His voice was deep and amused. 'I'm Inigo Webster, your grandfather. And yes, Arto is a wolf. Don't worry, he's just saying hello. We are both very pleased to meet you, Rowan. Come with me.'

And then his strong arms were lifting her and carrying her up the stairs. Over his shoulder, she watched the wolf padding after them, his eyes glowing golden in the lamplight. 'He looks like he's laughing...' she murmured.

'Well, people are quite funny,' Grandpa replied, setting her back on her feet in a cosy kitchen with wooden beams. There was a welcoming fire in the hearth. 'Sit there.' He pointed to the long wooden table with a

bench running along it, covered in soft red cushions. 'Welcome, my dears,' he said to them both. 'It's been too long.'

Rowan's mother put one arm through his, smiling up at Grandpa, as she blinked away tears of happiness.

Oh, so Mum got to be with her mysterious father she'd never even mentioned, she thought. What about how Rowan felt, missing her father? Part of her knew she wasn't being fair, but right now she didn't care. She sat down heavily, her eyes feeling gritty and tired. This was not her home and she did not want to be here. It was too dark and too quiet – apart from that strange noise Mum wouldn't talk about. And there was a big gap where her own father should be - she put her face in her hands so she didn't have to see it.

CHAPTER FIVE

ROWAN SAT THERE, HALF-DOZING, HALF-listening to Grandpa and Mum bringing in their bags and settling Peanut in the stables behind the house.

Arto came and put his head on her leg, fixing her with those bright eyes. He gave a small whine.

'Hello.' She stared

hard at the wolf. 'I suppose it's not your fault, is it? You probably don't want strangers in your house, either.' And she felt comforted by the warm heavy weight of his chin on her leg.

She was almost asleep when they came back in and Grandpa ladled out some hot soup.

Rowan dipped her bread into her bowl. 'How many animals live with you, Grandpa?' She yawned, trying to stay awake. She loved animals and she was never allowed to have any pets, back home in Holderby.

'Do they live with me, or do I live with them?' he asked, waggling his eyebrows.

She blinked at him, curious. She'd never thought of it that way round. And she'd never met anyone quite like him before.

'Don't tease her,' Rowan's mum told Grandpa, shaking her head and smiling. 'There's Arto and a horse

called Star. But every day, people bring their animals here to be healed, isn't that right?'

She looked at Mum sharply. How did Mum know so much? She must have been writing to Grandpa all along. So why hadn't she told Rowan any of this? She felt more determined than ever to discover the whole story. Starting right now.

'Are you a doctor?' Rowan looked at her grandfather, as he went to fetch a jug of water. She wondered how old he was. He seemed very tall and thin, tilting his head as he listened. He reminded her of the grey heron that used to fish in the palace ponds.

'You could say that.' He smiled again. 'But I help animals and birds, as well as people.'

'Can I help you?' she said. 'I like animals . . .'

'Arto can tell,' Grandpa said, looking at her intently with those deep brown eyes. 'He's a very good judge of character.'

Rowan smiled down at the wolf and stroked the thick fur of his neck. They stared at each other for a long moment. She sensed his loyalty, strength and courage.

Then Arto put his ears back, whined softly, and licked her hand.

The wolf liked her! For the first time today, Rowan felt a surge of hope. She had never met a wolf before. Maybe this new life wouldn't be so bad after all.

Her mother seemed to read her mind. 'It's going to be all right, Rowan.'

'Maybe,' she said, looking down at Arto again.

That deep, rumbling, thundery noise came again, louder than before.

Arto pricked his ears now and growled.

'What *is* that?' Rowan asked, grabbing at the wolf's neck for comfort.

Grandpa's face clouded over. He and Mum exchanged a complicated glance.

'What?' Rowan asked, looking from one to the other. 'I know it's not thunder. What aren't you telling me?'

'Living here, you'll learn about the Dark Forest,' Grandpa said gruffly. 'There are things you need to know.'

'What things?' she asked. 'Is it dangerous?'

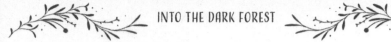

From the corner of her eye, she saw her mother give a very slight headshake.

'Not now, my love,' Mum said. 'It's time for bed. You can have a proper look round in the morning.'

Rowan huffed. They didn't trust her, that much was clear. They'd dragged her out here, to this strange place, and they weren't even telling her the truth!

But right now, she was too tired to argue. She stumbled after her mother. At the doorway, she looked over her shoulder.

She saw Grandpa putting on his coat and hat. He grabbed a bag from a hook by the door and slipped outside with Arto at his heels. Where was he going so late at night? Was it because of the strange sound?

Yawning, she promised herself again that she would start finding answers, as soon as she woke up. For now she plodded up the stairs after Mum, right into her own little attic room, which had just enough space for a bed and a wooden shelf to put her things on. Rowan unpacked her lucky feather, her shiny pebble and her animal book and arranged them on

the shelf. They looked lonely and out of place there. Like her.

Her mother kissed her head and said goodnight, taking the lantern with her.

For a few moments, Rowan lay awake, looking into the complete darkness and listening to the owls and the gentle creak of the house and the trees. And then she fell fast asleep and dreamed of a wolf made of stars, hunting through the night sky.

CHAPTER SIX

THE NEXT MORNING WHEN ROWAN WOKE UP, for a moment she thought she was at home. Then she remembered everything. She missed Dad so much that it hurt, right there in her chest. She waited till the homesick feeling eased, breathing in all the new sensations of this house. She looked at the sunlight pouring through the window and the steep wooden roof sloping above her. There was the warm scratchy woollen blanket pulled up to her chin, the scent of fresh bread and a slight hint of ... wet wolf?

'Arto!' She sat up.

The white wolf was sitting on the top step, watching her. His tail was wrapped neatly round his front legs, which looked damp, as if he'd been running in wet grass. Now he whined and came over to nudge her with his long velvety muzzle.

'Good morning to you, too,' Rowan said, smoothing her hand over his domed forehead.

His ears were outlined in darker grey, and his coat was thick and shaggy. Arto gave a wide yawn. With his jaws open, she could see his gleaming sharp teeth. He could rip a creature apart with those, but she felt utterly safe with him. Somehow she was sure that Arto had decided to protect her, though she couldn't say why or how she knew this.

The white wolf padded back to the stairs, paused, and glanced at her with his intense golden stare. *Hurry up,* he seemed to be saying. Then he went downstairs, his claws clicking on the wood.

'I'm coming!' she told him, and hurried to get dressed, pulling on her softest cotton shirt and some

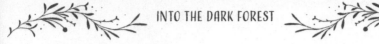 

old work trousers: clothes that wouldn't get spoiled if she went climbing in the forest.

Her mother was in the kitchen, going through a box of their things. 'Morning, Rowan. Did you sleep well?'

'Mmm-hmm.' Rowan went over and leaned against her mum for comfort, glad she was still here and still the same. 'I miss Dad,' she mumbled.

'Me too.' Mum's tone changed, so that Rowan could hear how much she meant those words.

'When . . . ?' Rowan's voice went all squeaky and stopped. She tried again. 'When will we see him again?'

'I don't know, love.' Mum hugged her tightly.

They stayed there for a long time without speaking. You couldn't argue with a war, Rowan knew. And it affected everyone, not just them. That didn't make it any easier to bear.

Eventually Mum said, 'There's breakfast...' and tilted her head towards the table, where half a loaf of bread waited, along with a small pot of plum jam. 'I made hot chocolate for you.' And she poured out a mug of frothy, creamy chocolate that made Rowan's mouth water.

'Thank you.' Rowan helped herself to breakfast and asked through a mouthful of bread and jam, 'Where's Grandpa?'

'Working.'

She could hear voices outside and went to peer through the back window. 'Out there?' Rowan asked. The house backed onto a large stable yard. It was tidy and well-swept, but only two of the stables were occupied. She could see Peanut looking out, curiously, and supposed that the large black horse in the next stall must be Star.

'He's got a workroom out there: he joined a couple of

the empty stables together, so it's roomy enough, even for the biggest...' Mum stopped, as her cheeks flushed pink. She picked up her mug of coffee, taking a deep gulp to hide her face.

Rowan noticed it all and didn't ask the questions that filled her mind. She knew that if you watched and listened, you could often learn more that way.

'Can I go down?' Now she was curious, instead of sad and homesick, and that felt like a good swap.

'Sure.' Mum sounded relieved. 'Leave Arto here and don't get in the way.'

Swallowing her last crust of bread, Rowan hurried down the back steps into the stable yard. Today she would start exploring and finding her own answers to all the mysteries of this new place!

The forest began just beyond the yard: tall beech trees loomed over the stable roofs, with their massive silvery trunks and the bright green leaves of early summer. The stable yard was a rectangle shape, with Grandpa's house and its trees on one side, and the stables on the other three sides, closing it in.

There was already a line of people waiting to see Grandpa. One had a goat; others had brought dogs, sheep and donkeys. Everyone turned to look at Rowan, and she felt awkward and self-conscious. The odd one out in this new place. Back home, she knew everyone's names, who was kind or grumpy or shy. Here, she knew nothing. Knew no one. She didn't like that feeling, and all of a sudden, she needed to escape.

Just then, Rowan noticed that there was a path leading from the far left-hand corner of the stable yard right into the forest.

Ah, so that was the quickest way into the woods! She peered longingly at the shadowy path. It seemed to call to her.

Right then, Rowan heard the rumbling noise again, the same as last night. What *was* that?

She had to find out. Rowan had a strong feeling that someone needed help. Just like she'd felt Arto hurrying her this morning. She was about to head towards it when a new idea struck her. What if there

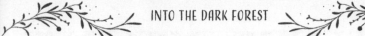 

was something dangerous out there? Surely Mum and Grandpa would've warned her, though? And if the grown-ups didn't trust her enough to tell her anything, she would have to explore by herself!

In a heartbeat, she made her decision, turned her back on the stable yard and the queue of strangers, and ran towards the forest.

CHAPTER SEVEN

ULL OF EXCITEMENT AND DETERMINATION, Rowan darted along the path and right into the Dark Forest.

Trees towered over her, their leaves filtering the light to make a soft green shade beneath their branches. Birds called. Creatures rustled through the tangle of grasses and thorny vines.

It was beautiful. As she walked through soft grass, dotted with flowers, Rowan had the strangest feeling that she had come home, finally. There were so many different trees arching overhead. She recognised oak

and beech and holly, and her namesake – the rowan tree. Right now the rowan was covered in beautiful blossom, but it would have red berries in the autumn. The name suited her, everyone said, because her hair was bright orange-red, the same colour as the ripening fruit, and her skin was creamy white, like the blossom.

She came to a clearing, edged in rocks.

Rowan sniffed. She could smell burning.

She saw that the bushes and trees at the far edge of the clearing had been scorched. Some branches were blackened; others hung down as if something had torn them off. 'What happened here?' she whispered to herself.

She turned slowly, seeing the damage to the trees, the crushed grass, as if something enormous had been dragged along the floor. There were even deep claw marks.

It looked as if something huge had been in a fight. But she knew there were no animals that big, except in stories. Then she remembered the loud noise she'd been hearing since they arrived, and the way Grandpa

and Mum had reacted strangely. What kind of animal made a sound like that, louder than a bellowing bull?

What weren't they telling her about the Dark Forest?

Just then, she spotted a patch of smouldering grass. Rowan put her hand out and felt the heat rising up from the ground. 'What could do this? I don't understand.' Again, she got the strangest feeling that someone needed help. Someone close by. Her heart started beating faster as she looked all around her.

There, by her foot, was a piece of eggshell. She picked it up: it was large and curved and emerald green. Too big to belong to any bird.

She walked round the edge of the clearing, trying to understand for herself what had happened here. Just then, she heard a noise, a bit like a squeaky door.

Mrrrr-eeeep.

She followed the sound.

It came again, something like a cat in distress.

She climbed a large rock, listening hard, and peered down behind it.

Rowan saw a flash of green scales. Was it a snake?

She bent down to look closer. 'Oh!' She recognised the creature from her story books.

A green dragon was staring back at her. It looked very small and very scared.

Rowan stared in astonishment, hardly able to believe what she was seeing.

CHAPTER EIGHT

THE DRAGON HUDDLED DOWN, LOOKING afraid. One of its wings was twisted. It made a hissing sound and tried to flap its wings. It must be injured, because it cried out even louder.

'It's all right, little one, I won't hurt you,' she told it.

Dragons were real! Amazed, Rowan drank in the sight of this magical creature.

The dragon was bright grass-green, covered in shiny scales. It had two long pointed ears, large yellow eyes and four strong little limbs, with tiny spines all down its back and tail.

Rowan felt a surge of protectiveness and love for the baby dragon. Without stopping to think, she reached down and picked it up, cuddling it close to her chest. With her free hand, she stroked the dragon's head. It felt cool and smooth. It blinked once and then closed its eyes.

'You're beautiful, aren't you?' she told it gently. 'I'm sorry you're hurt. My Grandpa's a healer,' she whispered. 'So maybe he can fix your wing. But first, let's try and find your mum.' She looked around for more signs of a large dragon. Which way had it gone? Remembering those claw marks, she began to retrace her steps.

She'd only just left the clearing when she heard raised voices. Rowan stepped behind a broad oak tree, staying hidden, and peered carefully through its leaves.

Just a few strides ahead, there were a handful of strangers dragging a huge net along the floor. These people were armed with spears, bows and arrows. They must be hunting, even though Rowan hadn't seen any deer or rabbits or pheasants today.

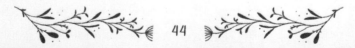

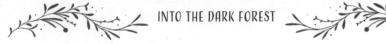 

'Hurry! It's not safe here,' one of the hunters was urging the others. 'We need to leave before the wildsmith gets us.' He looked very young and nervous, not much older than Rowan.

What was a wildsmith?

'Just do your job,' one of the others growled, narrowing his eyes. 'That's what Kaine Stonelaw pays you for.' That man had short hair and a bristly chin. His nose was an unusual shape, as if it had been broken in the past. He looked like someone who had survived many fights.

'Yes, Magnus,' the nervous boy said.

From their flowing robes and clipped accents, Rowan guessed they were Estrians, and the name Stonelaw sounded familiar.

Why didn't they feel safe? They were the ones with all the weapons! A wildsmith must be a fearsome creature indeed if these hunters were scared of it.

She kept very still. Rowan needed to find this baby dragon's mother and warn it there were hunters nearby. They were getting closer now.

She heard one of them saying, 'Faster! Our warriors will need the power from these dragon horns more than ever, now we are at war. We have to get back before nightfall . . .'

And, as they passed by, just the other side of the oak tree, Rowan finally realised what these people were doing. She saw what had happened to the mother dragon.

She felt sick. One hand flew up to cover her mouth so she didn't cry out. *Keep still,* she thought to the baby dragon, cupping it close to her chest and hoping it wouldn't give them away.

The Estrian hunters had a huge green dragon caught in their net. Its eyes were closed, but it was still alive: she could see its scaly ribs moving up and down as it breathed. There was a slender dart – a bit like an arrow but smaller – still sticking out of its neck. She could see its white-feathered shaft. The hunters must have used that to send it to sleep, so they could steal it away!

And yes, sure enough, it did have two huge gleaming

horns, there between its ears. Did they have magic powers? Rowan wished she knew.

The baby dragon squirmed in her arms, and she felt its distress. It was shaking with fear.

As the hunters got further away, she risked speaking again. 'Oh no,' she asked, 'was that your mother?'

And the little green dragon burrowed its head into her stomach, telling her *yes*.

Rowan held it tightly. 'I'll look after you, I promise,' she said. 'Let's hurry back and tell Grandpa what has happened. Maybe he can help.' With an aching heart, she hurried back through the forest.

CHAPTER NINE

ROWAN RUSHED ALL THE WAY BACK TO Grandpa's. He must have had a very busy morning because the line of people had gone. He was inside the stable talking to his last visitors.

Just outside, she noticed an empty handcart with a large blanket in it, covered in black and white dog hairs.

Rowan checked that the green dragon was hidden beneath her shirt. Then she walked through the doorway.

There was a sheepdog lying patiently on a high table.

Grandpa was leaning down to run his hands over the dog's large soft tummy, while a boy and girl around her own age watched him with anxious faces.

Rowan urgently needed to talk to Grandpa, but not in front of strangers! She'd have to wait till he was alone. Impatiently, she stared at the children.

'What's wrong with your dog?' she asked the boy, keeping her arms lightly folded so no one would see

the bulge in her shirt where the dragon was hiding.

The boy was a little taller than her, with short curly hair, light brown skin and very blue eyes. 'She's due to have puppies soon, but she hasn't been eating,' he said. 'Our Dad wanted us to get her checked.'

The girl looked a bit younger, with masses of black curly hair tied back in a thick ponytail. She had huge hazel eyes, set far apart, and freckles across her nose. She gave Rowan a quick smile, then went back to watching Grandpa.

Rowan watched too, growing curious in spite of her impatience.

Grandpa was working with a strange tool: a cup-like bowl round one ear, attached by a long soft tube to another cup-thing that he moved over the dog's stomach area.

He straightened up with a sigh, rubbing his back.

'What is it?' the boy asked.

'She's fine. But there's maybe eight pups in there. No wonder she didn't fancy breakfast. She's uncomfortable, that's all.'

'What should we do?' the girl asked next.

'Feed her small meals, more often than usual, the best food your parents can spare. Soon she'll be looking for a safe quiet spot to have her pups.'

'Eight pups!' the girl said, eyes shining. 'Come on, Meg, let's get you home.'

Grandpa lifted the dog back into her cart and the children settled her on the blanket, fussing and stroking her ears.

That was the moment when the green dragon decided to speak up.

Mrrr-eeep.

'What did you say?' the boy asked.

Rowan coughed, hoping that she could distract them.

'Who are you anyway?' The boy's voice had a challenge in it. If he were a dog, Rowan thought, he'd have his hackles raised.

She replied, trying to stay calm and hoping that the dragon would be quiet for a moment longer. 'We came from the city yesterday to stay with Grandpa.'

Grandpa looked down at her, his bushy white eyebrows drawn together in a frown. 'What have you got there, Rowan? Show me!'

The dragon poked its head out of her shirt, climbed along her shoulder and stood up, greeting Grandpa with another loud, enthusiastic *mrrrr-eeep!* But then it hissed in pain and sank back, sniffing at its injured wing.

'So much for staying hidden!' Rowan told it. The dragon was the size of a cat, and as heavy. It was struggling to balance, and she was filled with protectiveness for this little creature.

'What have you done to it?' the boy shouted. 'You know nothing! This is a baby and it is hurt. It needs its mother. Stupid city girl. It's not a pet!'

Rowan was shocked into silence, just for a moment. Then she yelled back: 'I know that! The hunters took its mother. I'm not stupid. I rescued it!'

Rowan and the boy glared at each other.

CHAPTER TEN

ROWAN HELD THE LITTLE DRAGON IN PLACE on her shoulder, still furious with this boy for thinking the worst of her.

'You actually saw hunters? This is not good.' Grandpa looked serious, coming closer and gazing down at the dragon.

'But they didn't see me!' Rowan described the people and their weapons.

'I did not know the poachers had returned.' Grandpa shook his head. 'Though I looked for them last night, when I heard the dragon's alarm call.'

So that's what the rumbling sound had been! And it had been calling for help again this morning. It also explained why Grandpa had gone out so late. 'What can we do to help, Grandpa?' Rowan asked, tugging at his sleeve.

'I can't tackle the poachers alone. We will need help. But first, let's see to this young one.'

Rowan wanted to snap, 'See?' at the boy, but she swallowed it down.

'Come on, Rowan,' Grandpa soothed her, putting his huge hand on her shoulder, and steering her back into the stable. 'Will and Cam, you'd better come too. Meg will be fine resting there.'

'Will!' the girl scolded her brother, behind them. 'You didn't give her chance to explain.'

'Right,' Grandpa said. 'Tell us what happened, from beginning to end.' He took the green dragon from Rowan and put it on the table.

While Rowan explained, Grandpa brought his face close to the dragon, letting it sniff him and touch his nose with its own.

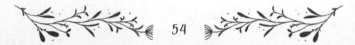

'There, now she knows me,' he said. And he checked the dragon all over, gently lifting its injured wing out to the side.

The dragon hissed again.

'I know, little one. It hurts, doesn't it?' Grandpa murmured. 'She must have broken this bone in her wing as she was getting away. See, Will?' he pointed, checking that the boy was watching.

Rowan looked carefully at the dragon's smooth green wing. It was so fine that she could see the tiny bones inside it, stretching out, a bit like extra-long fingers. And yes, she could see a little break in one of

the slender bones. 'I see it!' she said. 'The bone right at the wing-tip is broken!'

'Well done,' Grandpa said, 'that's it.'

The boy glared at her then. What was his problem? Maybe he was usually Grandpa's helper and he thought she was getting in his way.

It's not my fault, Rowan thought. *I didn't ask to come here.*

'I have some medicine to take the pain away,' Grandpa said. 'And I can put a splint on it, so it heals straight. I'm tired out, so we will do this the old-fashioned way.'

Rowan had no idea what he meant, but she watched, fascinated.

He brought out the medicine first, dripping some smelly, straw-coloured syrup into the dragon's mouth. Then Grandpa started gathering tools from the drawers that lined the far walls. He took out some lengths of cotton bandage, a knife, a pot of sticky vegetable glue, and an old feather. He trimmed the soft feathery parts so only the shaft was left. Then he glued this along the broken part of the wing with some soft pieces

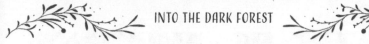 

of old cotton. 'The glue will dry and fall off as it heals,' he explained. It looked awkward, but the dragon didn't seem to mind.

In fact, the dragon seemed playful for the first time. She scampered up Rowan's arm and nibbled her ear.

'Hey!' Rowan laughed. 'That hurts! Try this instead . . .' and she dangled a spare bit of bandage for the dragon to chase.

The little green dragon batted the ribbon with her feet, rolling when she caught it.

'She's just like a kitten!' Rowan grinned, watching the green dragon play.

'Well, kittens and young dragons both need to learn to hunt. Dragons usually catch deer and smaller animals. They're predators after all,' Grandpa told them.

'Except when they're the prey,' Will said, looking very serious. 'What can we do to help, Wildsmith Webster?'

Rowan looked at Grandpa in shock. 'You're the wildsmith?' How could Grandpa be the person those hunters were so scared of?

CHAPTER ELEVEN

'W HAT, YOU DIDN'T EVEN KNOW THAT YOUR Grandpa is a wildsmith?' the boy asked, his voice dripping with disdain.

'I don't know what that is,' Rowan said, her cheeks burning. She hadn't even known she had a grandfather. And she certainly didn't know what a wildsmith was. Rowan felt so stupid, and she hated it. Back home, she was the expert on her city. The one who knew its secrets and shortcuts.

Here, she was like a newborn babe. She needed to learn, and fast.

Grandpa sighed. 'I didn't mean for you to find out like this.'

Rowan looked up at his kind face, already so familiar to her. She knew he was a healer. So why had those hunters been so scared of him? Suddenly she wasn't sure of anything.

The little green dragon came trotting across the table,

putting its head on Rowan's arm and blinking its yellow eyes.

She thought the dragon was comforting her, as she had comforted it, earlier that day. 'Thank you,' Rowan whispered. She stroked its back with one finger.

When she looked up, all the others were watching her in surprise.

'Are you a wildsmith too?' the girl said.

'No!' Rowan said. 'How can I be, when I don't even know what that is?'

'A wildsmith is a special kind of healer,' the boy said. 'Someone who can speak to magic animals and make them better.'

'Oh,' Rowan was relieved. 'But why were those hunters scared of you, Grandpa?'

'Those people don't understand,' Grandpa said. 'They're scared of a wildsmith's magic. Even though I only use it to heal. And these days, my power gets used up more quickly.' He sighed. 'But I do have knowledge and experience – I can use that at least, no matter how tired I feel.'

He did look tired, and older than before, Rowan saw.

'Hunters!' Will tutted at Rowan's choice of words. '*Poachers*, more like.'

Grandpa turned fierce then. 'The poachers come to the forest to trap the magical animals. They think that dragon horns will give them magical strength, but that's not true.'

'It's awful,' said the girl, Cam, looking at Rowan. 'They don't care that these are real, living animals.'

'And it's getting worse,' added Grandpa.

'We have to stop them!' Rowan cried.

'You are right,' Grandpa said. 'The war has made the poachers return. It's time we had help from our friends. I'll send word to the witches right now. We need to make a plan to stop them.'

'*Witches*?' Rowan burst out.

This time, Grandpa only smiled and shook his head. 'Will was right, you are a city girl!'

Rowan's head swirled with all this new information. She felt ready to burst with everything she didn't know: wildsmiths, poachers and witches.

Grandpa looked at the three of them standing in a row. 'It looks as though this little one is here to stay, till we find her a safer home. Will you children tend her for me today? She will need food, drink, warmth, and some playtime, if she is well enough.'

'Oh! Yes please!' the boy said.

Rowan felt a surge of jealousy. She had rescued the dragon. She'd brought it safely here. The dragon liked her, she was sure of it. Why did this stranger get to help?

'Thank you,' Grandpa said, nodding. 'I'm afraid I'm going to be needing your help more than ever, in these uncertain times.' And he went out, his shoulders stooped, as if he carried all the cares of the world on them.

Then Rowan was left with the girl and the boy.

The boy stared at her, and there was nothing friendly in his gaze.

She stared back. Why was this so hard? It wasn't hard at home. She and Bella knew how to make each other laugh, what each other's favourite foods were, how to tease each other out of the grumps and a hundred other things.

Eventually Rowan went for the obvious: 'What's your name?'

'I'm Willard. But people call me Will. And this is my sister Cam, short for Camille.'

'We live on the next farm,' Cam said. 'It's not far. Why don't you come with me, and I will show you round? I need to take Meg home and tell our parents that we are helping the wildsmith. But we can come straight back.'

Rowan didn't want to leave the dragon, but it wasn't for long and Grandpa obviously trusted these two. At least Cam was being friendly *and* she'd offered to show her around – that was more than anyone else had done!

Rowan had known her city friends for so long that she'd forgotten the beginning, the getting-to-know-you part. She smiled back, gratefully. 'Thank you. That sounds good.' She followed Cam, trying not to think of Bella and her old easy friendships back in Holderby.

CHAPTER TWELVE

OWAN AND CAM WALKED TOGETHER, BOTH pulling the handcart with Meg in it. It didn't take long to reach Will and Cam's farm, just down a lane and up the hill.

'Wow, is this your home?' Rowan stood still and gazed around. 'Lucky you.' She meant it. She could see a large farmhouse surrounded by barns, stables and sheds. They were built of pinkish-red brick that glowed in the sun, topped with old thatched roofs that looked to be softly laid over each building. There were fields spreading out along the edge of the forest, divided

by dry stone walls. Some fields were full of grazing cattle, others held sheep, and some had a patchwork of different crops. Growing up in the city, she'd never seen anywhere like this before.

'Thanks.' Cam smiled at her. 'We love it. Even if it's hard work.'

As they walked into a busy farmyard, Cam called out greetings to everyone they passed, leading the cart past a handful of roaming hens, two sleeping tabby cats and

a smiling woman in work clothes who looked so like Cam she must be her mother.

'Mum, Meg will be fine!' Cam explained what Grandpa had said about the sheepdog. Her words bubbled up: 'Will's helping Wildsmith Webster – please can I go back and help too? This is Rowan, from the city, and the wildsmith is her Grandpa!' she finished, laughing and breathless.

'Sure,' Cam's mum agreed, 'why not? Put Meg in that empty stall, till she decides where she's having her pups,' Cam's mum said. 'Hello, I'm Maddie.' She waved at Rowan.

Rowan smiled and waved back, liking Maddie straight away.

They wheeled the cart right into an empty stable. Meg the sheepdog jumped awkwardly down, scratched a nest in the straw, circled a few times and settled down to sleep. 'Rest now,' Cam whispered, stroking her soft ears.

Maddie appeared, holding out a bag of food. 'I know what it's like when Will helps the wildsmith –

he forgets to eat. Here's sausage sandwiches, cheese and herb pies and honey cakes.' She'd brought some juicy pieces of cooked meat for Meg the sheepdog. 'See you later! Much later, I expect.' And Maddie kissed her daughter's cheek and went back to work.

Cam took one of the pieces of meat that Meg didn't eat and wrapped it up. 'For the dragon,' she said, grinning. 'Will loves helping your Grandpa, but they've never had a baby dragon to look after before!'

As they walked back to Grandpa's house, Rowan tried to ignore the new and uncomfortable sensation of jealousy. All this time she hadn't even known about Grandpa. Now she did, she wanted to be the one who got to help him.

They found Will playing with the green dragon. Cam shared out the food from her mother and Rowan found she was ravenous.

'What shall we call her?' Cam said, giggling as the

green dragon shook a piece of meat and growled at it. 'We can't keep saying *the dragon* all the time.'

'Something green?' Will said. He seemed slightly more relaxed now.

'Moss! Apple! Leaf!' Rowan called out ideas, as she ate one of the delicious cheese pies and licked her fingers afterwards.

'Her wings do look a bit like spring leaves,' Cam agreed. 'Leaf suits her.'

'Leaf?' Will spoke to the dragon. 'Do you like that name?'

The dragon made a new growling noise, a bit like a purr. She flicked her tail from side to side and blinked her yellow eyes.

'She likes it!' Will said.

Rowan grinned. She had never named a real living thing before. She watched the dragon stalking Will's fingers, jumping on them and chewing them gently.

Will went to fill a bowl of water from the well in the yard.

Rowan twitched a stalk of stiff yellow straw in front

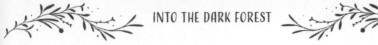

of Leaf. The dragon pounced on it, rolling over and over, and then biting it in two.

'Here, Leaf,' Will called, setting the bowl of water down carefully. 'You must be thirsty after all your playing.'

Leaf trotted over to the bowl, putting her nose right into it. She sneezed, sending water everywhere. Then she sat there looking surprised, her nose steaming.

'Steady, little one!' Will laughed and went back for more water.

'It's all right, you just made a splash,' Rowan told Leaf, stroking her back for reassurance.

She could see how gentle and kind Will was with the baby dragon. He was obviously just grumpy with new girls from the city. She chose not to take it personally, for now.

When she'd had a drink, Leaf yawned and curled up like a cat on some old sacking in the corner of the room. Rowan lifted her gently onto her lap so she could keep the baby dragon warm.

Then she looked at Cam and Will, saying, 'So, now

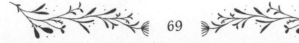

I know about dragons and wildmiths and witches and poachers, you'd better tell me the whole story.'

Will shrugged. 'I guess there's no harm, now you know that much.' He settled down next to her and began.

CHAPTER THIRTEEN

ROWAN HELD LEAF ON HER LAP AND LISTENED hard, ready to drink up every word.

In the old days, Will explained, magical creatures lived everywhere, but as people built more cities, the magical animals had retreated to the wild places, where they could still live in peace.

'But people cut down even more of the forests and built even more houses,' Will was saying. 'Now, the Dark Forest is one of the only places that dragons, pegasi, and all the other magical creatures are safe. Well, they were – until the war came closer.'

'What's a pegasi?' Rowan interrupted.

'Pegasus, you mean,' Cam said. 'A winged horse . . . You say pegasi when there's more than one.'

'Oh!' Rowan couldn't believe her ears. 'I can't wait to see those!'

'Hey!' Will said, 'I thought you wanted me to explain?'

'Sorry!' Rowan said. 'Just a few more questions: does everybody round here know about the dragons?'

'Our family, and your Grandpa, and our neighbours in Appledore village. We are the last keepers of the secrets of the Dark Forest,' Cam said next.

'And are you all wildsmiths?' Rowan asked.

'No, just your Grandpa,' Will said, giving her a sideways glance. 'But we know lots about animals from working on the farm. That's why he chose me to help him. Magic animals aren't so different. Usually.'

Rowan saw a mixture of pride and worry in his face when he said that. 'What about the witches? Are they scary?' Again she thought of pictures from storybooks.

Cam burst out laughing. 'No! They're kind. They're

powerful too, but they are our friends. And they look after all the animals, even ordinary ones.'

Rowan had more questions, but Leaf was waking up and that came first. She held the dragon gently as Leaf opened her eyes and gave a huge yawn. 'Hello you,' she said. 'Do you remember where you are? You're safe with us.'

Next, they gave her more food and drink, and played with her, till Rowan's fingers were covered in small scratches. 'Ouch!' she said. 'I'll wear gloves tomorrow!'

'We'd better go home,' Cam said reluctantly, as it started to grow dark. She and Will said goodbye to Leaf.

'Bye, little one,' Cam said gently.

'See you tomorrow, Leaf!' Will said, stroking her green head with one finger.

Then they waved to Rowan and were gone.

Left alone with Leaf, Rowan played chase with the baby dragon till they were both tired. Rowan sat back on her heels and said, 'Shall we go and find Grandpa now?'

Leaf growled sleepily and walked forwards, stumbling a little. She lifted her head, sniffing.

Rowan leaned forwards, on her forearms. Leaf touched her nose to Rowan's, blinking her golden eyes slowly, like a cat.

Rowan's heart melted. Leaf trusted her! 'I'm so glad I met you today,' she said. She might miss her father, her friend Bella, and her home in the city, but she had met Leaf, Cam and Will. If she tried hard, she could be friends with these new neighbours, she felt sure of it.

There was still no sign of Grandpa, so Rowan went to look for him. She carried Leaf with her, hidden under her shirt, just in case.

When she stepped into Grandpa's warm kitchen, she got her second shock of the day.

CHAPTER FOURTEEN

N THE KITCHEN, ROWAN SAW HER MOTHER, Grandpa and Arto, all sitting round the fire talking to someone, something . . . Who was that? *What* was that?

In the flickering firelight, the other person seemed to be made of shadows and light. They were moving, like smoke. They were made of flowers, of starlight, of flame. They were magic!

This must be a *witch*, she knew it.

'Rowan!' Grandpa stood up, making his chair scrape noisily along the wooden floor. 'I didn't see you there.

Well, come in and get warm. This is our friend Alyssa.'

Rowan blinked. Suddenly everything looked ordinary again. She must be tired, that was all.

This girl smiled at her. She was very beautiful, wearing soft orange robes, embroidered all over, and a garland of little yellow blossoms in her hair.

That must be why Rowan had thought of flames and flowers. She rubbed her eyes. 'Hello, Alyssa,' she said politely. Then she stopped. Should she hide Leaf? She kept her arms folded over her chest, just in case.

'It's all right,' Grandpa said, laying one huge hand on Rowan's shoulder. 'Alyssa is one of us. She knows.'

'I'm very pleased to meet you, Rowan.' Alyssa's voice was deep and rich and smooth as cream.

Rowan just stared at her. Something wasn't quite as it seemed. She didn't want to look away, just in case.

Alyssa stared back, smiling. Her skin was light brown, her eyes were amber in the firelight, and her thick black hair was loose, pouring down her back.

Rowan began to feel very scruffy, not helped by Arto, who came up and sniffed at her grubby shirt.

Leaf gave an alarmed squeak, and scampered right up her shoulders and neck, to sit on top of Rowan's head, chattering crossly and making all the grown-ups laugh.

'Ouch!' Rowan exclaimed, feeling foolish. 'Stop it, Leaf. Dragons' claws are sharp!'

Grandpa lifted Leaf off, and settled her on his own lap, though her tail spikes stuck up in fright and her eyes were bigger than ever. 'We were just talking about you, little one,' he said, stroking Leaf's green scales with one finger. 'Don't be scared of Arto the wolf. We're all friends here.'

Sure enough, as if she understood Grandpa's words, Leaf settled down, curling up, but keeping her eyes firmly fixed on the white wolf, just in case.

Mum beckoned, and Rowan was very happy to go and sit next to her, snuggling into her mother and trying to seem invisible so the conversation would carry on again.

Arto padded over and lay down at her feet.

'You were saying, Inigo?' Alyssa prompted Grandpa.

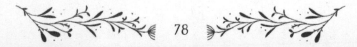

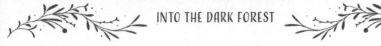

'You're sure the poachers are Estrian?'

'Sure,' Grandpa growled. 'They didn't even try to hide their presence. This war seems to make them more determined than ever to steal our magical creatures. Now they've destroyed their own forests, they want the creatures in ours!'

'I don't understand how they can hurt such beautiful animals,' Mum murmured, watching Leaf fall asleep again.

'They don't care. They think that dragon horns will give them strength and victory in the war.' He sounded angry and bitter. 'It's not even true. That's not how magic works.'

Rowan listened hard, determined not to miss a single word. She was actually learning about magic!

'How do we stop them?' Rowan's mother was asking. 'Should we fight them? Ask the queen to send some soldiers down here, too?'

Grandpa stared into the fire then, his hands still idly stroking Leaf's back, as he thought. 'Fight them: no. Stop them? Maybe. But Queen Silvana's soldiers are

busy defending the whole of Gallren from the Estrian attack. So we will need your help, Alyssa,' he said.

'My sisters are away, but I will summon them home. They will want to protect the Dark Forest, too, and we are stronger together,' Alyssa said.

She and Grandpa talked for a while longer. They made a plan that they could put into action when the other witches came back. 'Let's hope the poachers don't return till we are ready.'

Rowan listened, soon feeling drowsy in the heat of the fire, with Arto's warm chin resting on her feet.

When Alyssa finally stood to leave, she said, 'You know, Inigo, there's a home for Leaf, with us, when she's grown ...'

'But ...' Rowan squeaked and sat up sharply. 'Can't she stay here? We are her family now.'

Grandpa looked over at Rowan, and she could tell he was choosing his words carefully. 'No. I'm sorry, Rowan. It's not about how we feel. It's about what's best for Leaf. It's safer there, and there's more space. It's the perfect place for a growing dragon.'

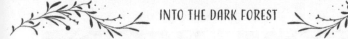 

'I don't want Leaf to go!' Rowan said. She'd only just met the young dragon, and now they were planning to send her away, with this stranger, with this *witch*!

As if she could read her thoughts, Alyssa smiled again and said goodbye to them all. 'I bid you farewell, for now. Thank you for calling me, Inigo. As soon as my sisters return, we will all take action together.'

And then, the strange shimmering smoke-thing happened again. One moment, Alyssa seemed to be walking towards the door. The next moment, she was gone. But the door hadn't opened.

Rowan blinked.

There was nothing but a small yellow flower on the floor.

CHAPTER FIFTEEN

'W HAT JUST HAPPENED?' ROWAN ASKED, open-mouthed.

Grandpa passed the sleeping dragon across, and laid her in Rowan's lap. Leaf seemed peaceful enough, but her scales looked a little duller than before.

'You met your first witch,' Mum said, and Rowan could hear the smile in her voice as she spoke. 'It's not something you forget in a hurry.'

'Witches! Wildsmiths! Why didn't you tell me any of this?' Rowan cried out. She felt cross with them all for keeping secrets. 'I thought magic was only in books

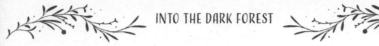 
and songs. Why didn't you say? You didn't even tell me about Grandpa.'

'As long as we lived in the city,' Mum said, 'you didn't need to know. It might've been dangerous. It wasn't what I wanted. It was best for you. And safest.'

'Why?' Rowan felt a niggle of worry then. She knew Mum wanted to keep her safe. Hadn't Mum always worried when Rowan played out till sunset or climbed too high? She might not like it, but it was one of the true and constant things in her life.

'Wildsmiths are rare. There are only a few of us left,' Grandpa said next, taking his turn to explain. 'We have a gift: for healing animals, and talking to them.'

'So Leaf did understand you! I thought she did!' Rowan cried out. Then she frowned. 'But why might it be dangerous?'

'The poachers want a wildsmith of their own, to work for them,' Grandpa said grimly. 'To lie to magical animals for them. To help them steal more magical animals. It's the opposite of what a wildsmith should use their gift for.'

'But that's terrible! Nobody would do that.' Rowan couldn't even bear to think about it. She looked down at the sleeping dragon in her lap, feeling so fiercely protective of her already. How could anyone hurt an animal? Especially one as beautiful as this. She made a silent promise – *I'll always look after you, Leaf.*

'Rowan, the poachers don't live by our rules. Their leader, Kaine Stonelaw, has awful ways of making people do what they want,' Grandpa said gently.

Rowan's head spun. 'I don't understand.' Her fingers reached out and touched Arto's warm body, leaning against her leg.

'What if the poachers had taken one of us, and threatened to hurt us, unless Grandpa did as they asked?' Mum said next.

'To save you, I would have no choice,' Grandpa told her.

'That's why we didn't tell you any of this,' Mum was saying. 'That's why we stayed away. We didn't tell you about Grandpa. About wildsmiths. About dragons. It was safer that way.'

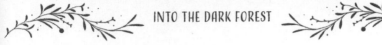

Mum went to Grandpa and hugged him, saying, 'I'm sorry, Dad. It wasn't easy for either of us, was it? At least we had our letters . . .'

'You didn't trust me!' Rowan was still hurt. Did they think she would go gossiping round the city, boasting about her magical family?

'It's not you we didn't trust,' Grandpa said, his eyes bright and flashing. 'But the Estrian leader is dangerous and deceitful. We wanted to keep you safe.'

'But it's not safe, is it?' Rowan said, shoulders tense, voice shrill, still careful not to disturb Leaf. She knew she wasn't being fair, but suddenly she'd had enough. She'd had enough of being carted around like a sack of grain. Of being lied to. 'It's not safe in the city. And it's not safe here. When that's the only reason Dad let us leave!' Her voice rose. 'So I could have stayed with Dad after all!'

'Shhhh, child,' Grandpa hushed her. 'You are still safer here. Stonelaw's army will try to take Holderby first.'

Rowan shivered. They still hadn't received a letter

from Dad. She tried to push away the worries that filled her mind then.

Grandpa was explaining, 'Only our friends and neighbours know I'm the wildsmith. Only those who live right next to the Dark Forest know its secrets. And they are all sworn to protect it.'

But Rowan was thinking about all the people she'd seen working on Cam and Will's farm. How Will had called Grandpa the wildsmith. It wasn't that much of a secret.

'Don't worry, Rowan,' Mum said, smoothing her hair and kissing her head, as if she was a small child still. 'Now, go on, up to bed with you. And Leaf can sleep there.' She pointed to a basket by the fire, lined with an old, soft blanket. 'It's late, and you look tired out after minding Leaf all day.'

Rowan found herself too exhausted to keep arguing. She put Leaf down gently and whispered goodnight to her.

'Rowan?' Grandpa said, as she headed for the stairs. She looked back at him, wearily.

'Thank you,' Grandpa said, his brown eyes warm and soft. 'You did well today.'

That helped. She nodded back, and felt the tension easing in her shoulders. She went upstairs, thinking hard, barely noticing the white wolf following.

But when she got changed and crawled under her blanket, Arto whined softly, then jumped up and settled himself on her feet.

'Oh. Is that your place now?' she whispered. She was

glad. She felt safer with him there, his heavy weight keeping her feet warm.

But her dreams were full of shadows and smoke, of huge unseen creatures chasing her faster, faster, faster through the dark woods.

CHAPTER SIXTEEN

THE NEXT MORNING, ROWAN WOKE UP AT dawn, feeling restless. She got up and tiptoed down the stairs, leaving Arto asleep on her bed. She looked at the doors opening off the hallway. That one was Grandpa's bedroom. That one was Mum's bedroom. So what was this one? She tapped at the door. Then she pushed it.

It creaked open, and swung inwards. Rowan stepped inside and gasped.

This room was like the inside of a nut, all polished wood. One of its walls was actually a living tree! She

darted over and ran her fingers over the curving trunk. The other three walls were lined with bookcases, following the natural curve of the building, stretching up above her head.

'Wow!' she whispered. 'It would take my whole life to read these . . .' She gazed at all the books, their spines lettered in crimson and gold.

'That's about right,' Grandpa said, startling her. There were two comfy armchairs in the centre of the room, around an iron cylinder she guessed was some kind of stove, with a large lamp standing behind each. He was reading in the nearest chair, with a thick blue blanket over his knees. 'Morning dear, couldn't you sleep either? Well, choose a book and join me, will you? Dragonlore is over there . . .' he gestured vaguely at the eastern wall.

'Really?' Rowan couldn't believe it. The city school had one shelf of books for everyone to share. This was breathtaking. She took her time, tilting her head to read the titles, till she found one that made her heart leap in excitement. 'This one's called *Dragons of the Forest*!

Oh! I can read that and find out more about what Leaf needs! She looked a little pale last night.'

'Yes, yes. Don't yip. Too early for that,' Grandpa grumbled, pulling his blanket higher and frowning under his bushy beard.

'Sorry!' Rowan whispered, curling herself up in the other chair. That morning she read and read, till Leaf climbed the stairs all on her own to remind the humans that it was breakfast time.

Will and Cam came over after breakfast and found Rowan and Leaf sitting by the fire in Grandpa's kitchen. Mum had already gone to market in Appledore, the nearby village.

'We came as soon as we could – we've never done our chores so fast!' Cam sounded breathless and her cheeks were pink. 'How's Leaf?' She settled herself on the floor next to Rowan and bent down to stroke the dragon's scaly green head.

'I think her wing is healing,' Rowan said. 'And she was so hungry this morning. But she is still a little pale, don't you think?'

'We brought more meat,' Will said, taking a package out of his bag and putting it on the table.

'Not there!' Rowan had discovered just how sensitive the dragon's nose could be.

Too late: Leaf had already smelled it. She got up and spread her wings and started trying to climb up the table leg, making eager little noises. So they gave Leaf her third breakfast, and washed their fingers afterwards.

'Where's Wildsmith Webster?' Will said.

'Working,' Rowan tilted her head towards the back window and Cam went to look at the busy stable yard where there were already three people waiting for Grandpa's advice. 'I guess most of his patients are ordinary animals?'

'And people too,' Cam said. 'He's the nearest thing to a doctor, round here.'

Her last words were lost as Rowan gave an enormous

yawn. 'Sorry! But guess what I read this morning in Grandpa's library?'

'He let you into the wildsmith library?' Will looked shocked. And hurt.

'Well, I let myself in, and he was there.' She hurried on. 'Anyway, I read that Leaf needs to play a lot, eat a lot and sleep a lot, to get stronger. But there's something else too: she needs firestones. Her mother would have gathered them in her mouth and brought them to her.'

'What's a firestone?' Cam asked, and Rowan was relieved she wasn't the only one who hadn't heard of them before this morning.

'Dragons need them as part of the fire-breathing process.' Will sounded like he'd memorised that in a lesson. 'And to grow properly. They crunch up the firestones and the stonedust helps them to ignite flame and to digest their food, I think.'

'Yes!' Rowan was excited by her discovery. 'They're found in the forest, in rocky clearings. The stones are formed within the rock, so you have to get them out.'

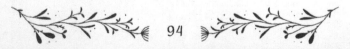

She told them what she'd read about how firestones were chiselled out of the rocks. 'That must be why Leaf and her mother were in the clearing. The poachers must have known it too, and waited there to catch her.'

Cam looked concerned. 'But if Leaf needs the firestones to be healthy and we don't have any, what will happen to her?'

'We'll just have to get some for her. We're in the perfect place to find them!' Rowan smiled broadly, waiting for them to share her excitement.

Will scowled and she felt a wave of frustration. Why was he acting like a spoiled child? Wasn't Leaf more important than anything?

'So, let's go look!' Cam said, noticing Will's silence and nudging her brother. 'We have to give Leaf everything her mother would've done, don't we?'

Rowan was glad of a reason to go back to the forest. She felt drawn to it in a way she couldn't explain. But she was tired and she had no time for Will's sulking today. She thought fast, settling on a plan: 'Will, why don't you wait here with Leaf, since you're usually

Grandpa's helper?' She still felt a stab of envy as she said that. 'Me and Cam can go to the forest and find the firestones. It isn't far. Grandpa and the witches seem to think the poachers won't be back for a while.'

This way she got to go into the forest again, and she wouldn't have to see Will's resentment written all over his face.

Will looked suspicious, but Leaf crawled onto his lap, as if she'd understood exactly what Rowan was suggesting, and the green dragon distracted him.

'Ah, don't fuss, big brother!' Cam patted his arm. 'You know you want to stay here and have some time with Leaf on your own.'

'Well, that's true,' he said, stroking Leaf's head.

Rowan took an empty backpack from the hook, and rummaged in Grandpa's tool basket for a large chisel. 'Bye, you two. We won't be long.' She hoped that was true, as she took one last look at Will and Leaf sitting together in front of the fire.

Then Rowan and Cam tiptoed down the back stairs, across the stable yard and into the forest, without being seen by Grandpa who was still busy in his workroom. Rowan got the feeling he wouldn't be happy about her going into the forest. But she could be there and back with the firestones before anyone even noticed they were gone.

CHAPTER SEVENTEEN

'TELL ME MORE ABOUT THE POACHERS,' ROWAN asked Cam, once they were underneath the green canopy of the trees once more. 'Have you ever seen them?'

'No!' Cam said, her eyes round. 'They've never come so close before! It's because of the war, my parents said. But we've heard about them from Wildsmith Webster.'

Before Rowan could ask more, she heard a rustling in the bushes behind them. The girls jumped apart, alarmed. Rowan's chest felt like it had a dragon flapping its wings inside it.

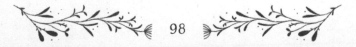

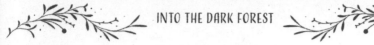

'Who's there?' Rowan called out, her voice shaking slightly.

Suddenly she saw how foolish they'd been to come back to the Dark Forest, unarmed and alone. Alyssa didn't expect the poachers to come back so soon. But what if she was wrong? What if they hadn't even left yet?

A pale feathery tail appeared, waving above the ferns.

'Arto!' Rowan felt her legs grow wobbly with relief. 'I'm so glad it's you.'

The white wolf came and pressed himself against her, growling softly.

Rowan had the strongest sense that he was scolding her for coming into the woods. 'Well, we had to get the firestones for Leaf,' she said, defensively. 'Will you come with us and keep us safe?'

Arto looked up, golden eyes narrowed. He whined and pressed his damp nose in her hand.

Rowan was sure he was asking her to come home. She told him, 'I'm determined to do this.'

Arto sneezed in disapproval, but he padded ahead of Rowan, sniffing the air as he went.

'Look! He's showing us where to go,' Cam said.

They followed Arto's lead, and before long, they were back in the clearing where Rowan had found Leaf.

Using the chisel she'd brought along, Rowan started chipping away at the rocks, till she could see the veins of reddish-gold inside, just as the book had described them.

'Look, Cam! That must be the firestones.' She tapped at the rock and gently dug with her tools. 'A mother dragon must use her claws and teeth for this,' she said. Finally, some of the firestones came away. They were shiny and reddish-gold, like little stone berries. 'They're so beautiful!'

They worked until they had a small pile of firestones.

'That should be enough for Leaf to crunch up – she's only small,' Cam said, gathering the stones into their bag and slinging it on her back. 'We can always come back for more.'

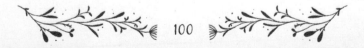

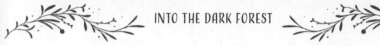

Rowan dusted her hands down and got ready to leave.

Just then, Arto growled and stood tall. The hackles on the back of his neck were raised. Every inch of his body looked ready to run or fight.

Then the girls heard it too: an animal bellowing in fear and pain.

Rowan did not stop to think. She answered the call for help. She ran straight towards the noise, leaving Cam with Arto.

She ran faster than she'd ever run in her life, jumping over fallen trees, pushing through ferns and thorns, rushing till her breath came fast and hot.

There! Just ahead, through the trees, she glimpsed an enormous dragon: a huge red scaled creature, bigger than the tallest horse, wider than three carts. It was magnificent. It was roaring, fighting, bellowing.

It was surrounded by poachers, the same ones as before. They were armed with spears and bows and arrows. But they hung back, wary and cautious. They didn't dare get close to an angry adult dragon.

'Cowards!' Rowan whispered, with tears in her eyes.

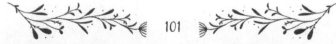

Then she saw one of the poachers lift a blow-pipe to his mouth. It was the man with the broken nose. She saw his bristly cheeks grow round as he took a huge gulp of air.

Thwooot!

With a sharp puffing noise, the dart flew out of the pipe – she glimpsed its white feathers as it sped – straight and strong.

It pierced the scales of the dragon just below its throat.

Again, the dragon roared.

Then it crashed down onto the earth and didn't move.

Rowan stopped, heartbroken.

She was too late.

Worse, she was all alone and in terrible danger.

CHAPTER EIGHTEEN

ROWAN HOPED THAT ARTO HAD STAYED WITH Cam to protect her and lead her home. She crept forwards, wishing her heart wasn't pounding so fast and so loudly. In spite of the danger, she needed to see what the poachers were doing. She peered through the trees.

The poachers were busy now. She could hardly bear to look as they bundled the sleeping dragon into their net, ready to take it away. It was huge, twice as long as a large carthorse.

Suddenly, a thought struck her: what if this dragon

had been protecting its nest, just like Leaf's mother? A strange certainty, deep inside, told her she was right.

Rowan didn't know how she knew, but she did: there was a nest of dragon eggs nearby. She could almost feel them. It was a strange kind of knowing, like a tug in her mind. She had to reach them before the poachers did.

She looked around, barely moving, trying to guess where the dragon might have nested. It would be a large space, so the dragon could brood its eggs, protected from rain and wind.

Rowan spotted the perfect place: just to her left, where an old sycamore tree had fallen against a tall rock. Staying hidden, she crept closer, listening hard all the time.

'Rowan!' Cam hissed.

Oh no! Rowan spun round. Arto and Cam had both followed her. Now they were all in danger and it would be her fault if anything happened to them!

She put her finger to her lips and mouthed the words: 'Poachers! They've taken a red dragon. I'm searching for its nest.'

'No!' Cam shook her head, desperate. 'Too dangerous!' she mouthed. 'We must go!'

'You go.' Rowan felt stubborn. 'Just one moment. That's all I need.' And without waiting for an answer, she tiptoed sideways towards the nest.

Hardly breathing, she parted the ferns and looked down: yes! She was right.

There, on the floor, was a dragon's nest, with a cluster of four pale pink eggs. She bent down, holding her breath, and lifted one egg, then another. She put one in each pocket. Then she picked up the other two, and slowly, slowly, moved backwards, retracing her steps back to Cam and Arto.

'Here! Can you carry these?' she whispered, handing over two eggs to Cam. 'Let's go!'

They all turned to leave, just as Arto growled a warning.

Rowan peered over her shoulder, and her heart stopped. The poachers were coming! She saw them: five strangers, heading towards them, searching for the nest as they came.

'Run!' she said, not caring who heard now. 'Run!'

Rowan fled from the poachers, praying that she wouldn't smash the eggs. She could feel them in her pockets, bumping up and down. She heard Cam and Arto, just behind her.

An arrow whistled through the air. With a *thwack*, it embedded itself in a tree trunk, just an arms-length away.

Faster! She pumped her arms, pushing onwards.

Then, to her horror, Grandpa's white wolf stopped running. Arto turned to face the poachers. He was giving the girls time to escape.

CHAPTER NINETEEN

'ARTO, NO!' ROWAN CRIED. SHE CHECKED again: now he was crashing through the bushes in the opposite direction. The white wolf was leading the poachers away – giving Rowan and Cam the chance to escape. She had to trust Arto now.

Please be careful, Arto! Rowan thought in desperation. She was getting tired. She didn't want to lead the poachers straight back to Grandpa's house. What could she do?

Then it hit her: what did she always do? *She climbed.*

She might not be in the city any more, but she was still Rowan. Climbing was her best chance now.

She looked around. Yes! Right there stood the perfect tree: a broad oak with leafy branches that would hide them. The lowest branch was chest height. They could do this.

'Cam! We have to hide,' she explained fast. 'They're too fast for us. And we mustn't lead them back home. Can you climb?' she gestured at the tree.

'Of course I can!' Cam said, looking as determined as Rowan felt.

So Rowan turned, gripped the first branch and lifted herself up. It was hard, because of the eggs. She had to move more slowly and carefully than usual, when every instinct told her to rush. Her palms were slippery and hot. She made herself breathe, deep and slow. You can do this, she told herself. Our lives depend on it.

Her hands and feet fell back into the old rhythm, finding the next branch, the next foot-hold, the next hand-hold. She looked down: Cam knew what to do, she saw with relief.

Soon, they'd climbed into the upper branches. Rowan wedged herself close to the trunk on a wide branch. She glanced down, through the leaves, checking that they were well hidden.

'If we stay here long enough, they'll think they've lost us,' she whispered to Cam, just below her, hoping it was true. She could feel the eggs in her pockets: still whole, still safe. 'They will want to get back to the sleeping dragon in case it wakes.'

She put her face against the rough bark of the tree trunk, listening, over the pounding of the blood in her ears. Beyond the rustling leaves, she could hear the poachers, calling to each other, getting further away. Slowly, birdsong returned to this part of the forest, telling her it was safe once more. She prayed that Arto had got away.

Rowan and Cam waited till the light was beginning to fade. Then they climbed down, even more slowly, because they were stiff and cold.

Rowan looked around in despair: they'd run so far that she had no idea where they were.

She had never felt further from home. They were lost. She had no idea where Arto was. She'd wanted to help, but she'd only made things worse. Now the poachers would know they had the eggs. They would come looking for them. She'd just made things more dangerous than ever, for these eggs, for her family, and for Leaf.

CHAPTER TWENTY

OWAN HATED NOT KNOWING THINGS. BUT right now she was perfectly happy to admit it. She felt very relieved when Cam took charge and led them safely home.

At Grandpa's house, they found Mum, Grandpa, Will and Maddie waiting in the kitchen, looking pale and anxious. And Arto, looking very pleased with himself for getting home first.

'I'm sorry!' Rowan burst out. 'It was my fault, not Cam's.' She could see they were in for the scolding of their lives. 'Arto helped us get away.'

The mothers unleashed their feelings:

'What were you thinking of?'

'You could have been killed!'

'We feared the worst!'

That was just the start of it. Even Leaf joined in, chittering away from Will's shoulder.

Rowan looked at her feet while the shouting happened, one hand on each egg, waiting for her moment to explain. She knew Mum only worried because she loved her, but Rowan hated upsetting her.

When their scolding was over, Rowan said, 'Now can we show you what took so long? First this.' She put the firestones in front of Leaf.

The green dragon immediately took one in her teeth and started crunching on it happily. Rowan was sure that Leaf's green scales gleamed more brightly as she ate her first firestone.

'But more importantly . . .' Rowan lifted the eggs from her pocket. 'Grandpa – the poachers hadn't even left yet! They took the red dragon, but can we still save her eggs?'

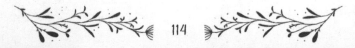

'Quickly, we must warm them by the fire.' Grandpa hurried to build a soft pile of cushions for them, and the girls laid the eggs down in their strange new nest.

Then Grandpa looked sharply at Rowan. 'How did you know they were there? Wasn't the nest hidden?'

Rowan remembered the strange feeling that had led her to the eggs. 'I'm not sure. I just knew.' Over the past months, this had been happening more and more – strange new instincts she couldn't explain.

She saw the look her mother gave Grandpa then: a mixture of hope, excitement and fear.

For three days, Rowan wasn't allowed to leave the house. She didn't mind this punishment, she was so busy playing with Leaf, feeding her firestones, and

watching the nest of pink dragon eggs. Arto didn't leave her side.

But she missed Cam, who had been given extra chores back home at the farm. Will came to visit and check on the eggs.

'I am sorry,' Rowan jumped straight in before Will could speak. 'It was reckless and stupid, and Cam might've got hurt.'

'Yes,' he said, twisting his mouth in a rueful smile, 'But I probably would've done the same thing.'

Rowan smiled back, feeling something shift and change between them.

'Look,' he said, 'the wildsmith lent me this.' He took out the book about dragons. 'It says that when they are ready to hatch, you can hear the baby dragon moving and tapping inside the egg. It's the same with our hens' eggs when the chicks are ready. Shall we listen?'

Leaf squawked and went to sniff at the eggs. The green dragon had been very interested in the eggs from the moment they appeared. Now she flapped her wings in excitement.

'Careful, Leaf! Your wing is still healing, remember?' Rowan told her.

Leaf only stretched her neck and made little high-pitched *ee-eee-eee* sounds.

'It's time to turn the eggs anyway,' Rowan said, 'so we can listen while we do that.' It was one of their jobs, to tend the eggs like the mother dragon would have done. They had to keep them warm, and slightly damp, and turn them regularly, so no part got cold.

Now Rowan lifted the first egg carefully up to her ear. She held her breath and listened.

Was it still alive?

Tap-tap-tap.

'Yes!' Rowan gasped. 'I heard something.'

CHAPTER TWENTY-ONE

 OWAN GENTLY PLACED THE EGG BACK IN the nest, being sure to rotate it. 'You try, Will!'

With his blue eyes shining, he took the next egg and lifted it. 'I think so! Not tapping exactly, but I heard it moving. They're getting ready to hatch!'

'We have to fetch Cam!' Rowan said. 'Do you think your parents will let her come, now? But hurry, you don't want to miss the hatching!'

'I'll go and see. We should have time – with chicks it can take a while.' Will hurried from the room.

 118

Rowan, Arto and Leaf sat round the nest of pink eggs and waited. Will and Cam came back. They waited. And they waited.

They waited all that day.

Still no new dragons.

Finally Mum persuaded Will and Cam to go home, and Rowan to go to bed. 'They'll hatch when they hatch,' she said. 'You're doing a good job, but exhausting yourselves won't help.'

Rowan built the fire up, turned the eggs again, then trudged up the stairs to bed, with Leaf sitting on her shoulder like a tame parrot. She yawned. 'Wake me, Arto. Please? If they hatch, wake me up?'

In the still, silent hour before dawn, Arto came and licked Rowan's cheek.

'Yuck, wolf drool!' she said. And then she remembered: 'Is it now?'

Arto thumped his tail, his mouth hanging open as if he were grinning.

'They're hatching? Oh!' Rowan ran down to the kitchen and fell on her knees by the nest.

The first egg was already cracked: she could see a little hole where the baby dragon had tapped at the shell.

'Come on, little one!' she said. And then she realised it would need food. She dashed around, filling a small dish with water and two plates of shredded chicken: one for Leaf and one for the baby dragons.

It all happened very fast then. Before she knew it, the eggs were being tapped open from the inside and the baby dragons were crawling out. They seemed very tired and slightly damp and sticky.

'Oh! Hello! I'm so pleased to meet you,' she greeted them. She dripped water into each little snout and dangled pieces of meat for them. 'Here, eat this.'

Leaf was helping. The green dragon crawled from one to the other, acting like a big sister and nudging them towards the meat, growling gentle encouragement.

One by one, each of the baby dragons revived enough to gobble down some food. Leaf showed them how to preen, as Leaf's mother must have shown her, licking her feet clean and smoothing her scales.

By the time the sun came up, there was a sleeping tangle of dragons: one large green and four small reds.

'And they all fed and drank water – are you sure?' Grandpa was astonished. 'How did you manage all on your own?' he asked, when he came downstairs, yawning.

'I wasn't on my own,' Rowan told him, puzzled. 'The dragons hatched, and then Leaf and I worked together.'

Grandpa looked at the sleeping dragons. Then he looked at Rowan. Back and forth, back and forth. 'Hmm,' he said. 'We'll have to test my theory, but . . .'

'But what, Grandpa?' Rowan was used to grown-ups being a bit vague in the mornings. Coffee usually helped, she'd found, so she poured him a big cup, added milk and honey, and passed it over.

'I might not be the only wildsmith left in our family after all,' he said.

'Oh! You mean me?' Rowan froze where she stood. 'A wildsmith?'

Her first thought was pure joy. Her second thought was for Will – if it were true, he would be very angry indeed.

CHAPTER TWENTY-TWO

OULD ROWAN REALLY BE A WILDSMITH? She hadn't even heard the word before they came here. Was Grandpa right? It was true that Leaf usually knew what she meant. And she and Arto understood each other perfectly. Rowan thought back, finding more and more examples from her life here and in the city over the last weeks and months. She was so happy, she felt like a fire had been lit in her heart, burning more brightly with every passing moment.

'A wildsmith knows a wildsmith,' Grandpa said, nodding. 'It often begins to show at your age. Though

I wasn't sure till now.' He took her small hand in his huge one. 'It's a big responsibility,' he told her gravely. 'And a huge gift.'

'I want to be a wildsmith, like you,' Rowan said seriously, meaning every word. 'I want to protect the magical animals. All animals.' She was still worried about the poachers returning.

'Good,' Grandpa said, 'because it's not exactly a choice, I'm afraid.'

Then Cam and Will were knocking at the door, full of news of their own. 'Meg has had her puppies!' they said, at exactly the same moment as Rowan said, 'The eggs have hatched!'

They made so much noise laughing and talking over each other that Grandpa took himself off to the stables with another cup of coffee, grumbling, 'I'd forgotten how much noise human pups make! You know where I am if anyone needs me.'

Rowan watched him go, feeling like a bucket of cold water had been thrown over her. When would he tell Will the truth?

The next few weeks were the busiest of Rowan's life. The poachers didn't return and she almost stopped worrying about them. She would have been happier than ever, except for missing Dad. It was like tooth- ache, always there in the background. You could forget if you kept busy, but as soon as you stopped, it came back. As soon as you woke up, it was there. She thought that it must be the same for Leaf, missing her mother, and it made her love the green dragon even more deeply.

She divided her time between the dragons in Grandpa's kitchen and the eight puppies on Will and Cam's farm. At first Meg's pups were just like furry squeaking sausage rolls, feeding and sleeping the whole time. But they grew quickly, till they were tumbling and growling and tripping over their own paws. Soon there was so much to do, playing with all the new animals, training the puppies, feeding the dragons and watching them grow.

Leaf adored her new foster brother and sisters. It was

lovely to watch the red dragons copying her clumsily, as they learned to chase, crunch firestones, flap their wings and bite each other.

The dragons loved Arto too, reaching up to his shoulder now, following him around the kitchen, trying to play with his feathery white tail. Soon, the five young dragons seemed to fill the whole room!

The day came when they learned to fly. Rowan ran in from visiting the farm, to find Mum sweeping up a pile of broken pottery shards.

'That,' Mum said dryly, 'used to be your Grandpa's favourite mug.'

'Oh,' Rowan said. 'Oops.'

'And I was brewing some cough mixture, before the dragons decided to taste it,' Mum pointed to the saucepan that had been tipped over on the stove, with sticky claw marks showing who had done it.

The red dragons were perched in a row along the back of the bench. They seemed to know they were in trouble. They folded their wings, tails down, ears drooping. They did look very sorry.

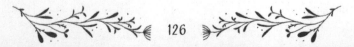

'You didn't mean it, did you?' Rowan said, going to stroke each one's neck, the way they liked it.

They'd named the dragons for reddish fruit, to match the different shades in their colour. Strawberry was the large bold one with bright red scales. Plum was the tiny fierce one with purple-red scales. Raspberry was the quiet one who loved cuddles, with pinkish-red scales. Bramble was always the last one to be found, the one who never wanted to stop playing, and her scales were dark aubergine colour like blackberries.

Now they all crowded round Rowan, flying up and roosting on her shoulders and head. 'Ouch, you're getting too big for that!' she told them, with a heavy heart. She knew it was true. This kitchen was too small for them. One day soon they would need open space. They would need to fly freely and practise hunting. If she loved them, she had to let them go.

Mum met her gaze with kindness and understanding. 'They need more room. It's nearly time, isn't it, love?' she said. 'I'll tell Grandpa to contact Alyssa.'

Rowan's eyes filled with tears. The dragons might be nearly ready, but she wasn't.

But when Grandpa came in, he said something that took Rowan's breath away. 'You might be right: the dragons will soon be ready for their new home. But first, they've got an important job to do. They're going to help us stop the poachers. Alyssa has been tracking them and they're headed this way again.'

Rowan embraced her dragons, trying to ignore the fear that swirled in her heart.

CHAPTER TWENTY-THREE

HEN ROWAN WAS PLAYING WITH THE dragons that evening, she found the room shimmering with heat-haze once more. This time, Alyssa had brought her sisters. When the air cleared, there were three witches sitting round the table with Grandpa and Mum.

One witch had very white skin and hair like snow, tumbling down her back like an avalanche. The other had very short hair, black as the midnight sky, scattered with jewels like stars. Her skin was dark brown, and her eyes were topaz.

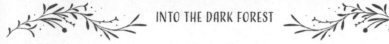

'These are my sister witches,' Alyssa introduced them: 'Mara.' The snow-witch nodded. 'And Safira.' The star-witch smiled.

The dragons were drawn to the witches, hopping onto their arms and shoulders. The witches didn't flinch – though Rowan knew how sharp those claws could be! They greeted the young dragons warmly.

'Hey, beauty,' Alyssa said, stroking Raspberry under the chin, where her pink-red scales faded to cream.

'Will you help us?' Mara asked Strawberry, while Plum tried to hunt the witch's long elegant fingers, almost knocking over the milk jug.

'It's time to stop those poachers who took your mama,' Safira told Bramble, who pawed and bit at the golden bracelets she wore.

'How can they help? They're only young!' Rowan rushed in, wishing she could grab the dragons out of their arms without seeming rude. 'I don't want to put them in danger!' she said.

'And yet, you ran in to save them without a thought for your own safety,' Mara turned her piercing green eyes

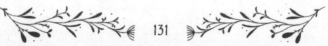

on Rowan now. 'And some would also call you young.'

'Well, that was my choice!' Rowan said. 'I had to save them.'

'And this will be their choice,' Safira said, gently. Her large brown eyes were like deep golden pools, and Rowan couldn't look away.

'We have a plan,' Grandpa told Rowan. 'And you can also help. Would you like to hear it?'

Rowan glanced at Mum then, expecting her to say it was too dangerous, that Rowan had to stay safely at home. But Mum only bit her lip. Rowan could almost see her wriggling with the effort of not saying those things.

'Of course I want to hear it! If we can stop the poachers stealing any more animals, I'm in!' she said, plonking herself on the spare chair, and putting her elbows on the table. 'Tell me the plan.'

The witches laughed, and it was like the noise of the wind in the trees.

'I think we're going to need more tea,' Mum got up to put the kettle back on the stove top.

The next morning, they set out at dawn. Cam and Will had been disappointed to be left behind, but Grandpa would not be moved on his decision. The sky was pearled blue-grey and the air was cool and full of birdsong. Grandpa and Arto led the way through the Dark Forest. Rowan came next. Five dragons followed. Nobody spoke.

She knew the plan. They'd stayed up late going over and over it.

The witches explained it carefully to the dragons, and Grandpa checked they understood.

Rowan felt strange and light, as if her legs were made of cotton and her head was made of dandelion fluff. It was just nerves, she told herself, but she couldn't help worrying that this was too much to ask of such young dragons.

They reached the place they'd agreed: a large clearing dotted with firestone rocks, and a likely place for a dragon to nest.

Alyssa, Mara and Safira were already there.

'Look!' Alyssa pointed at the ground in front of them.

'See, there?' Mara pointed to a square of netting on the floor between them. If you didn't know it was there, it was almost invisible. Each corner had a loop of stiff rope attached to it.

Rowan's stomach did a somersault when she saw it. She hoped the first part of the witches' plan would work, and they wouldn't need this after all.

'Are you ready?' Grandpa whispered to Leaf.

Leaf nudged Grandpa's chest with her scaly head, and then leapt into the air. She flapped hard and started circling in the misty sky above them. She was the lookout. She would let them know if the poachers grew near.

Alyssa vanished, heading east.

Mara vanished, heading west.

Safira vanished, heading south.

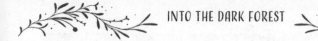

They were going to find the poachers and use their magic to entangle them. The dragons would only get involved if they failed.

Now there was nothing else to do but wait.

CHAPTER TWENTY-FOUR

OWAN AND HER GRANDPA EACH TOOK TWO of the young red dragons and found a hiding place. They would keep the dragons warm and feed them with dried meat, to keep their strength up in case they were needed.

Rowan's stomach was fizzing now. It wasn't just anxiety, there was excitement there too. She was working as a wildsmith. She was doing something important. She would be making a difference to all the magic animals of the Dark Forest.

Sitting in the lowest branches of an oak tree, Rowan

held Plum, the smallest and fiercest of the dragons; and Raspberry, the sweet quiet dragon. Plum was full of energy. She didn't want to sleep or rest. Supple as a weasel, she wound her way round Rowan's neck, down her back, under her jacket, along her arm.

'Hey, shhh! You're supposed to be saving your energy!'

Plum blinked her yellow eyes at Rowan.

'Oh, are you nervous too?' Rowan asked. 'It's not easy, sitting here waiting.'

Plum grew calmer then, as if she was reassured by that. She folded her wings and settled around Rowan's shoulders, just under the hood that hid her bright red hair. Raspberry curled up like a cat on Rowan's stomach.

The sun came out and the air grew warmer. Flies buzzed around Rowan's face but she didn't brush them away. It was as if she'd turned into a tree herself.

Just when her feet started to fall asleep completely, they heard it. Leaf's alarm call, high above in the pale-blue sky.

The first part of the plan hadn't worked! Where were the witches? What had happened to them?

'Stay here, Rowan,' Grandpa said, in a stern, quiet voice. 'Leaf says the witches are injured. I'll go and see if they need my help. Keep Bramble and Strawberry near you. I'll take Arto.'

'All right,' Rowan whispered back. 'Good luck!' She heard Grandpa's rustling journey through the woods, leaving her all alone with the dragons.

For a time nothing happened.

Then Leaf called again, louder and nearer this time.

Rowan understood her perfectly.

People are coming. Poachers are coming! And Rowan was the only person left in the clearing.

The fear almost won. She could stay hidden, wait for Grandpa, and hope the poachers didn't see them.

But they had a plan. Why shouldn't it work? Grandpa would be back soon, she was sure of it.

So Rowan took a deep breath, calling all her power in. It was up to her and the dragons now. They had to stop the poachers and protect the creatures of the forest. She could do this. She had to do this. If she didn't make the dragons understand, they would all be in terrible danger.

'Plum! Raspberry,' she whispered. 'It's time. Remember what we planned? Bring the poachers right into the clearing. And keep out of their range. I believe in you.' She pressed her lips to Plum's flat little head, feeling the cool scales, then dropped a kiss on Raspberry's head too.

Then the red dragons slipped away and down the tree trunk, using their claws to cling to the bark. They

darted across the clearing and flapped their wings, launching into the air.

Plum and Raspberry met their nest-mates in the clearing. They flew as if they had no cares in the world, just four young dragons playing and chasing each other. They spun in the air, turning circles, above the witches' net.

Right there, in full view of the poachers who'd crept closer and closer, their weapons ready.

Her beloved dragons had become the poachers' next target.

Rowan held her breath.

CHAPTER TWENTY-FIVE

THIS PART OF THE PLAN WAS THE MOST important. Without seeming to notice the poachers, the dragons flew slowly backwards, drawing them into the clearing. Strawberry dived on Plum, in their game of chase. Raspberry darted after Bramble. It looked completely natural.

Not at all like a trap.

Just then, Rowan spotted motion to her right. Without moving her head, she glared from the corner of her eye.

Today there were only two poachers, the same ones

as before, dressed in cloaks and flowing trousers, hats pulled low.

They tiptoed noiselessly forwards, hunting the dragons.

Hunting *her* dragons! She clapped her fingers over her mouth so she didn't make a sound. *Keep flying,* she thought to the dragons. *Keep drawing them in.*

The poachers were good, she'd give them that, even the young one who still looked scared. They moved without making a sound, ducking under branches, stepping over twigs that might've snapped and given them away.

The young one had an arrow drawn and nocked, in a strange, small bow, quite unlike those used by the royal guards back home. Suddenly he stopped and asked, 'Shouldn't we go now, before those witches come back, Magnus?'

Rowan saw that his hands were shaking.

'This won't take long,' the broken-nosed man replied. 'You hit that witch back there – good shot. Now let me get these, and we can be away. Stonelaw will be

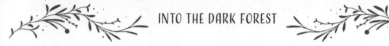 

very pleased if we bring all these young ones too.' He had his blow-pipe ready, loaded with a feathered dart.

Rowan felt an icy shiver then, knowing what he planned. She shuddered in dread. How could anyone do that?

She watched her dragons dance up into the air, catching the first rays of sunlight: dazzling, beautiful.

Still the poachers crept forwards, their eyes on the dragons.

They didn't look down. They didn't see the net.

Then the plan stopped working. Plum and Bramble weren't as fast as the others. They were still within reach of the poachers' weapons.

She saw the young poacher boy stop and take aim, so close she could see the tendon in his neck, the tension in his trembling fingers, about to release.

She had to do something, or he would shoot.

Plum! Bramble? Hurry! You need to fly out of range, Rowan thought frantically. But they still weren't as fast as the other two.

She couldn't sit still and watch it happen.

This scared boy wouldn't dare hurt her, she felt sure of it. Sure enough to take the biggest risk of her life.

With a burst of hot fury, Rowan ran forwards, out of her hiding place. She turned to the poachers, so they could see her face, see she was a child, unarmed and defenceless. She wanted to distract them long enough for her dragons to move away. *Get further back,* she thought to the dragons again in desperation, and then she ran backwards too, hoping the poachers would chase her.

She had to time it just right.

Every moment, she expected to feel an arrow in her back, but she ran forwards, gathering speed.

Yes! They were coming after her.

She only had a few paces left: three, two, one.

Then she leapt: flinging herself up, avoiding the net, jumping higher than she'd ever jumped in her life.

Yes! She caught the branch with her right hand, hanging there, fighting to bring her left hand up, arms burning.

Finally, both hands gripped the branch, and she

used her momentum to swing up, one knee over the branch, till she lay gasping on her tummy.

Below her, the first poacher stepped onto the net the witches had laid.

Keep coming, she thought.

Just long enough for the other one to step on, behind the first.

Rowan focused hard. They had to act now, before it was too late.

Now, she thought to the red dragons. *Grab the corners and lift!*

The four red dragons dived down, so fast that the poachers had no time to react to this strange behaviour. Each red dragon grabbed the loop of rope in their claws and flapped hard, lifting up, up, up.

The plan was working!

Rowan saw the net curving up around the poachers. She saw them struggling through its mesh. *Ha*, she thought. *See how you like it, being caught in your own net.*

'Yes! My brave dragons!' she cried.

But then, disaster struck. Plum dropped her corner of the net – she wasn't as big as the others.

The loop fell down and the net flopped open.

The broken-nosed poacher leaned out, his blowpipe still in place, aiming straight at Plum.

'No!' Rowan shouted. 'Look out, Plum! He's going to shoot you!' If anything happened to these dragons, she would never forgive herself. What kind of wildsmith was she, if she led her friends into danger?

CHAPTER TWENTY-SIX

IME SEEMED TO SLOW DOWN FOR ROWAN then, as she watched the poacher aiming at Plum. She wanted to help, but there were only moments left. The man sucked in air and prepared to blow.

Then there was a flash of bright green. Something whizzed across Rowan's vision. 'Leaf!' she gasped. 'Oh, be quick! Get that corner!' she told her.

Leaf flew in and seized the loop in

her claws. She grabbed and lifted it faster than Plum had been able to.

Again, the dragons flapped their wings. This time they tugged the four corners of the net up off the ground and right into the air.

The poacher lost balance, and huffed the dart out as he fell. It hit the other one, who screamed and brushed it off, and then they were both tumbling together. Their arms flew up. Their weapons fell down. An arrow snapped. Hands flailed in the air, trying to catch hold of anything solid, finding only netting.

The dragons worked hard, flying up, straining to hold the rope. Plum was helping Bramble with her corner. Together, they were strong enough to lift the captured poachers. But Rowan could see how tired the dragons were.

Just a little longer! She thought to them. *You're doing so well!*

Working together, the dragons took it in turns to hook each loop round a short stubby branch high up on a sturdy oak tree. The net dangled there, secure at

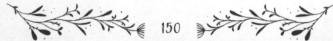

last, and the dragons' task was done. They glided to a nearby branch and sank down, exhausted. Their wings flopped, flat and limp, and they rested their heads on each other.

The poachers cried out in shock and anger. The more they struggled, the more the net squashed them together. One arm poked through the mesh, then someone's leg. It looked awkward and uncomfortable, but quite safe. They were cursing and swearing at Rowan and the dragons..

Slowly, aching and sweaty, Rowan wriggled along her branch, catching her clothes on every twig and knot. The fiery energy had left her, and she struggled down, feeling tired and clumsy, finally reaching the ground once more.

Suddenly the witches appeared again, dotted around the net.

They were all injured. Alyssa was bleeding from a deep gash on her arm. Mara had a trickle of blood running down her face. Safira was limping as she approached.

'What happened?' Rowan called. 'Are you all right?' If these two poachers had managed to hurt the witches, they must be more powerful than she had feared.

CHAPTER TWENTY-SEVEN

ROWAN GAZED AT THE WITCHES IN CONCERN, wondering how badly they were hurt.

'Don't worry! We'll be fine,' Alyssa called.

'They fought dirty, but we are stronger,' Mara shouted.

'It's only a scratch, but it interrupted our spell,' Safira explained. 'Long enough for them to escape.'

Stay back!' Alyssa called a warning next. 'Keep away from them, in case their weapons can still be used. We need to finish this.'

For their plan to work, they needed the poachers alive. Alive and uncomfortable.

Alyssa tossed up a waterskin. 'Make it last.'

Mara spoke next: 'We'll let you out this time tomorrow.'

They would spend a day and a night dangling there. They would be cold and hungry – but not thirsty, at least.

Safira finished: 'Then you will return home and make sure all the poachers hear this.'

The three witches spoke together: 'Tell everyone the Dark Forest is out of bounds. These magic animals are under our protection. If you return, we cannot guarantee your safety.'

The power in their words sent a shiver down Rowan's spine. There was magic in that command.

The Estrian poachers did not speak. They had got the message, loud and clear.

Now it was safe, all five dragons flew down from their branch, curious, but wary.

The dragons were free. The dragons were safe.

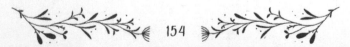

Grandpa appeared next to Rowan. 'Don't you ever do that to me again, child. We were supposed to stay hidden. When there is a plan, we stick to it!'

She felt his strong arm round her shoulders, and she turned and hugged him tightly. 'We did it! It worked!'

Grandpa's eyes still looked worried. 'That last move was pure recklessness. I saw you through the trees. I thought my heart would stop.'

'But they were going to fire an arrow – the dragons might've been hurt!'

'You might've been hurt!' Grandpa shot back. Then he calmed a little. 'But you were doing well till then, young wildsmith. The dragons trust you, and that made them fearless.'

The dragons swooped down now, making high-pitched noises, landing on Rowan all at once, so she fell over, swamped by proud happy dragons.

'Argh!' she giggled as they romped across her tummy and legs. 'Yes, you're all very clever dragons – but that tickles! Stop!'

Five dragons seemed like a lot more, as they nibbled and squeaked and hopped around, celebrating their success.

'Come along, all of you,' Grandpa said. 'I think we all deserve a huge second breakfast. The poachers aren't going anywhere.'

Arto threw his head back and howled, and it was a cold eerie noise that travelled far and wide.

Alyssa moved one arm in a sweeping gesture and suddenly the net seemed to vanish, leaving the clearing looking empty and untouched.

'It's a glamour,' Mara explained, seeing Rowan's puzzled face. 'They're still there, but the enchantment stops anyone seeing them or entering the clearing while it isn't safe.'

'And it stops them climbing out,' Safira said with satisfaction.

'Oh!' Rowan decided there and then that she would never get on the wrong side of a witch.

'Now, let me see those injuries,' Grandpa said, going over to tend to their wounds. 'Rowan, you come too. It's about time you saw a healing.'

Rowan watched, entranced, as Grandpa started working on Alyssa's injured arm. He was using his wildsmith magic!

She was astonished to learn that she could see it happening! She stared. Would she be able to do this one day? Her mouth fell open.

Rowan could actually see the healing, like a stream of golden light, bright as the sunrise. She could see it flowing up from the earth, through Grandpa's whole body, like water through a paper straw. It flowed right down to his fingertips. Then the light disappeared into the injured arm, so it knitted itself back together again. He did the same for Mara and Safira.

Afterwards, Grandpa was very tired. He leaned on Rowan's arm as they all walked slowly back through the forest with Arto and the dragons.

When they arrived at Grandpa's house, Cam and Will were waiting, and jumped up asking questions all at once. Mum had been distracting herself by cooking the biggest pile of blueberry pancakes that Rowan had ever seen.

'Dear dragons!' Cam said, 'Here's your breakfast!' And she put down a huge bowl full of fine meat scraps.

Grandpa sank down into his chair, groaning, 'I'm a weary wildsmith. I'm getting too old for this sneaking out at dawn malarkey.'

'Hush, Dad. You're not old. You're brilliant,' Mum said, as she handed out huge mugs of coffee to Grandpa and the witches. 'Well done, everybody!'

'Well done the dragons, more like,' Rowan said through a mouthful of pancake.

And the rest of the day was spent eating and talking and sleeping – humans and dragons all needed naps. Whether witches did, Rowan was too tired to wonder.

CHAPTER TWENTY-EIGHT

HE NEXT MORNING, ALYSSA THE GREEN-WITCH returned in a flurry of golden flowers, finding Rowan and Grandpa in the stable yard tending to Peanut and Star. Arto was dozing in the sunshine nearby, and the dragons were sleeping in one of the empty stables, all twined together in deep straw, still tired after all their hard work the day before.

'The poachers have gone,' Alyssa told them firmly. Her arm looked completely healed. 'We sent them back with a deep ... *commitment* to spreading the word. The Dark Forest should be safer, from now on. So, didn't

you say these dragons needed more space?'

'Already?' Rowan said, trying to keep her voice steady. She knew it was the right thing. The dragons would have the perfect home with the witches. It would have enough space – and enough firestones – for them all. And she'd seen the way witches understood dragons. Her beloved dragons would have everything they needed. Still, her heart clenched with sadness. 'Can I at least tell Cam and Will to say their goodbyes?'

'Here they are now,' Grandpa said.

As if summoned by Alyssa, the four red dragons and one green dragon came sleepily trotting out of the stable, just as Will and Cam wandered in from the forest path.

Rowan crouched down, hugging each dragon in turn, even though they were so big and heavy now she could hardly lift them any more. She started with Plum. 'I love you, little dragon,' she whispered. 'Keep growing well. Keep crunching your firestones and practising your flying. You're so beautiful. And I'm so proud of you.' And then, as the tears started dripping off her chin,

she let Plum go to Cam and she went to hug Bramble. Raspberry was next, and then Strawberry.

When it came to Leaf, Rowan could no longer speak. She knelt on the floor and opened her arms.

Leaf came to her, wrapping her long neck around Rowan's and leaning her head on her shoulder.

Rowan held the green dragon close to her heart and hoped Leaf could tell what she meant. She hoped she could feel the love flowing from her heart.

Leaf made a little *mrrrrrpp* sound and pulled back so they could gaze into each other's eyes, one last time. Leaf blinked slowly with her golden eyes.

Then she leaned forwards.

For a long moment they rested, forehead to forehead. No words were needed.

'It's time,' Alyssa said. 'Dragons? Come with me!'

The witch beckoned and the dragons drew close to her, each finding a point of contact on Alyssa's body.

Next time the witch-shimmer happened, all of them vanished.

Rowan blinked away tears. Only Grandpa stood there now, and Will, and a tear-stained Cam.

'Oh,' Rowan said, as her heart swelled with sadness. Arto padded over and sat down so close that his thick fur tickled her nose and made her sneeze. She wrapped both arms around his neck and hid her tears in the pale fur.

'Your first success,' Grandpa said, his voice kind and warm. 'The first magic animal rescue. Not the last, I'm sure. For now, take the time you need to be sad

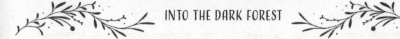 

and miss your dear dragons. But one day soon, it'll be time to look forwards. There are always more animals needing help.'

Rowan nodded, and let Arto lick the last tears from her cheek.

CHAPTER TWENTY-NINE

THE HOUSE SEEMED VERY EMPTY AFTER Alyssa had taken the dragons to live with her.

Rowan started helping Grandpa in the mornings, and doing lessons with him in the afternoons. She noticed that he sometimes used wildsmith magic, but at other times he used ordinary knowledge to heal and bind up injuries. Grandpa said Rowan was too young to practise a healing. It could be dangerous because of the way it drained the wildsmith's energy. But she used her gift for speaking to animals every single day,

welcoming or distracting or calming all the animals Grandpa helped.

Grandpa had finally told Will that Rowan was a wildsmith and, after avoiding her for a few days, he seemed to accept the fact. Rowan still visited Cam and Will every day to play with the puppies, but they were growing too, and soon each one of them had a new home to go to.

As summer faded, Rowan's homesickness returned. She missed her father more than ever. She wondered what Bella and her other friends were doing in Holderby. She was desperate for news of the city. She found herself moping around, unable to settle to a task.

Mum noticed. 'What you need is a change,' she said, after she found Rowan slumped in her chair one morning, playing with her piece of toast instead of eating it. 'I've talked to Grandpa, and he agrees. It's your birthday next week and we've arranged a surprise trip.'

'Really?' Rowan sat up straight, scattering crumbs

everywhere. Maybe they were going home! Maybe she'd get to see Bella again – and Dad!

'Really.' Mum laughed and hugged her tightly, murmuring into her hair. 'You deserve it.'

Rowan's birthday was a perfect sunny day in late summer. She even received a letter from Dad – knowing he was safe was the best birthday present. After a special breakfast of pancakes with honey, they all set off together. Grandpa rode Star, and Rowan, Mum, Will and Cam were in the same cart that had brought them from the city, pulled by Peanut. The steady chestnut mare found a new burst of energy, determined to keep up with Star's long strides.

'Where are we going?' Rowan kept asking. She turned to Cam. 'Do you know?'

Cam mimed a buttoning motion over her mouth. 'I'm not telling! It's your birthday surprise!'

It took hours, but they finally arrived. Along the way, Rowan realised they weren't going home to Holderby. She tucked her disappointment away deep down, and focused on enjoying the day.

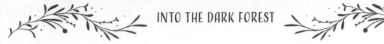 

'There!' Grandpa pointed with one gloved hand.

In the misty distance, Rowan could see a hill topped by a slender tower rising up from the forested slopes around them. The road spiralled up, wrapping itself right round the hill.

It was perfect. It was breathtaking.

Then she spotted firestone rocks, dotted across the grass. Her heart leapt with hope.

'There? Is that where we are going?' But her question wasn't answered by anyone human.

Five dragons were prowling outside the tower, sniffing the air. Then, at the same moment, they all took flight, flapping huge leathery wings.

'Look! It's our dragons!' Rowan shrieked in delight. She turned to Mum and hugged her. 'Oh, thank you! Thank you! Thank you for my birthday present!'

Leaf rose up first, high into the air above the tower, with the four smaller red dragons chasing her.

'Oh, there's my Leaf! There's Plum. And that's Bramble. That must be Raspberry, or is it Strawberry? They've changed so much ...!' Rowan cried out, shading

her eyes and staring. 'Look how big they are! Bigger than Arto! They're getting almost as big as Peanut! Hurry up, Peanut, hurry!'

Mum picked up the reins and urged the mare on.

The dragons showed off their new flying skills, swooping low and calling out greetings, then turning

somersaults in the air, diving right down and recovering at the last moment.

'Hello, hello! Oh, I missed you! Aren't you fine? And so huge!' Rowan couldn't wait. She tumbled right off the cart and ran as fast as she could up the hill, chasing the dragons all the way to the top.

She lifted her arms, waving and laughing, trying to drink in the wonderful sight of her dragons, so free, and so happy here.

It was a bittersweet joy, to see them flying free, soaring over the green valley. They were better off here, but she still missed them!

Alyssa came out to greet them: one moment the empty space shone and pulsed, the next moment she was standing there, smiling and welcoming them to her home.

Rowan wondered if you ever got used to it, witches appearing and disappearing like shadows on a sunny day.

'Welcome, and Happy Birthday, Rowan,' Alyssa said. 'I've prepared a feast for us all.' And she gestured to a table set for six, groaning under heaped dishes

of delicious-smelling food, and a huge, tiered cake decorated with whipped cream and plum syrup and fresh, juicy blackberries.

The next thing Rowan learned about witches was that they were wonderful cooks; soon there was nothing left but crumbs.

While Mum, Grandpa and Alyssa chatted about all the affairs of the wider world, Rowan and her friends played with the dragons for hours.

'You're taller than me now!' Rowan told Leaf, measuring herself against the green dragon. Their shoulders were at the same level, but Leaf's strong supple neck curved high over Rowan now. 'I remember when I could lift you up!'

Cam and Will started laughing. 'You sound just like our grandma.'

Rowan laughed too. 'I do feel a bit like their mum, or their big sister at least.' She moved between the red dragons, stroking their ears and patting their scales. 'Look how beautiful they are. I feel so proud of them!'

'We did a good job, didn't we?' Cam said, scratching

between Strawberry's ears, just how he liked it.

'These dragons are safe from the poachers, and when they lay eggs, we'll protect them too.' Will sounded determined.

The dragons grew hungry and restless, and they flew down to the forest to hunt. The setting sun caught their scales as they soared away, making them blaze like jewels.

When Rowan had promised to look after Leaf, she hadn't realised that would include giving her up. But she could see with her own eyes, it was the best thing for all the dragons.

Rowan watched them till they were tiny specks in the clear sky. Then she smiled at Cam and Will, seeing the same complicated expressions on their faces: pride and joy and sadness.

'Come on,' Mum called them back to the cart to start the long journey. 'It's time to go home.'

And Rowan found that, for the first time, she was actually thinking of Grandpa's house on the edge of the Dark Forest as her home.

All the way back, she dozed and daydreamed, wondering which magical animal they would help next.

THE END

ROWAN'S ADVENTURE CONTINUES IN

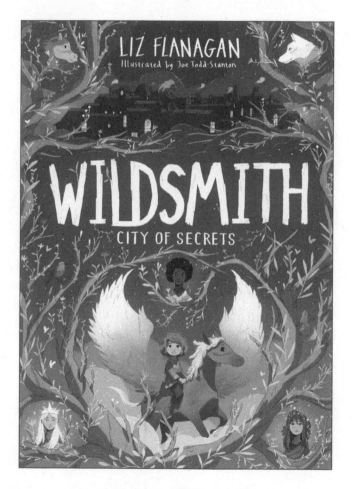

COMING APRIL 2023

ACKNOWLEDGEMENTS

Huge thanks to my agents Abi and Phil for suggesting I write a magical middle-grade series in the summer of 2020. It was a lovely escape for me during those strange months. Thanks to everyone at UCLan for being a dream to work with, especially Tilda, Hazel and Becky. Thank you to Joe for these magical illustrations. Thank you to the fantastic children's books community of bloggers, booksellers, librarians and readers. And to all our foster animals: thank you for your fine company, for the fun and for all you taught us, I hope you are thriving in your forever homes!

IF YOU LIKED
THIS, YOU'LL LOVE . . .

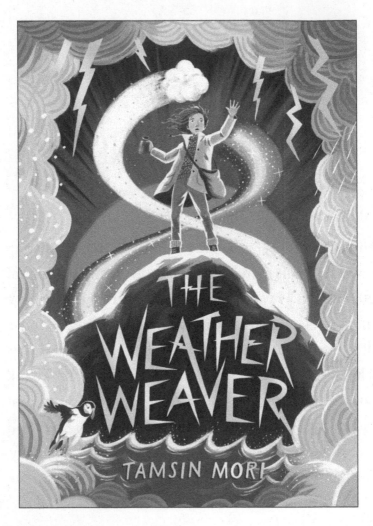

THE
WEATHER
WEAVER

TAMSIN MORI

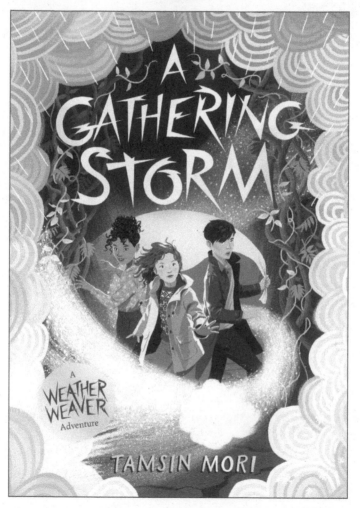

A GATHERING STORM

A
WEATHER
WEAVER
Adventure

TAMSIN MORI

AUTUMN MOONBEAM

DANCE MAGIC!

EMMA FINLAYSON-PALMER & HEIDI CANNON

AUTUMN
MOONBEAM
★ SPOOKY SLEEPOVER! ★

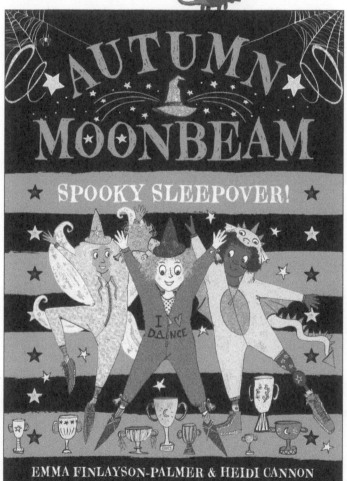

EMMA FINLAYSON-PALMER & HEIDI CANNON